Mail Order Bride

The Reluctant Duchess

by

Rosemarie Sabel Durgin

Writing Rose Press
Bethany, Ok.

This is a work of fiction. Any resemblance to people living or dead is purely coincidental. The village of Novorotskoye does not exist.

No part of his book may be reproduced in any way, either manually or electronically, without the written permission of the author and publisher.

ISBN-13:987-0692867723
ISBN-10:0692867724

Rosemarie Sabel Durgin

Also by Rosemarie Sabel Durgin:

The Kinder Castle

Coming Soon:

Women, Immigrants, Pioneers

Rosemarie Sabel Durgin

MAIL ORDER BRIDE

THE RELUCTANT DUCHESS

Mail Order Bride

DEDICATION

This book is dedicated to my Writing Group, Creative Quills, and all our members. I thank the El Reno Carnegie Library for making it all possible, and for the support they have given us, since the inception. Thank you, Penny Beals, and Alishia Ballard. Thank you, Debbie Fogle, Tuna Dobbins, Carol Nichols, Shawn Smith, Julie Marquardt, Sue D. Smith, Glenda Brown, Chuck Baker, Susan Jacobson and Johnna Kaye for all your inspiration and support.

My most heartfelt thanks go to our leader, Professor Andrea Foster for without her, this book would never have happened. Thank you for teaching me, cajoling me, inspiring me, and most of all for being my friend and editor.

I would also like to thank the staff at Canadian Valley Vo-Tech. Without your support and guidance this book would never have happened. The courses you have offered have been most helpful for me. Thank you all so much.

Most of all I want to thank my husband John for all the help and support he has given me. Love you!

In memory of my mother, who instilled in me my love of books and reading, from an early age.

And of Uschi, my faithful companion and protector for fourteen years. I miss you terribly.

Mail Order Bride

Chapter One

K atja came home that day, hungry, wet and cold. It had been a miserable day. They had been replacing worn trestles on the railroad line to Yekaterinburg. Her friend Olga met her in the hall of the dacha.

"This big letter came for you today. It has some unusual writing, and the stamps are very different too. Oleg thinks it is from America. Who do you know in America?" Katja shook her head, she knew no one in America.

She took the letter and walked up to her attic rooms. She changed into her warm robe and then settled herself in the one comfortable chair in her rooms and with the letter opener that once had belonged to her great grandfather, she cautiously slit the top of the letter open. There were several pages written in English and Katja settled down to read what was written.

Ekaterina:

This letter is in response to your picture and proposal in a magazine. I hope you have not received another proposition which you have accepted. This letter is to introduce myself and to invite you to join me here in America, and to also inform you of what I am able to offer you. I am going to be as honest as I can, so you can form a better judgment, but I am speaking about myself, so I might unwittingly paint my picture rosier than a third person might.

My name is Clifford Collins and I live in the far northwestern corner of Oklahoma, just a few miles from both the Colorado and New Mexico border and about fifteen miles from the county seat and the only town around, Boise City.

I am going to be fifty-two years old on my next birthday in a couple of weeks. I am 6'4" tall and weigh about 220 lbs. I am neither fat nor skinny. I carry that weight well on a large frame. My doctor is satisfied with that weight. He also tells me I am surprisingly healthy for my age. I used to have dark blond hair, but it is full of grey, what is left of it, that is, and I do have blue eyes.

I speak and understand a little Russian. My grandparents came from Russian stock, but I am afraid I do not write it at all, and I am also wondering, if it is not archaic since the folks came over before the turn of the century. My suspicion is that it is also heavily laden with English words. But I think, we should be able to communicate. Hopefully, you know some English. If not, perhaps you can have a few lessons before you come over. I will pay for that expense.

In fact, let me know how much money you will need to settle your affairs. I am willing to send you the funds. Also, how much do you need for travelling expenses? I will mail you the tickets to get here. Tell me where you live and how you expect to get to Moscow or St. Petersburg for Airline flights to the West. I will obtain those tickets also. If another International Airport is closer to you, let me know. I will arrange things from here.

As I understand it, a visa is no longer required for a visit to the United States for tourists and you will arrive here under that status. We will have to be married within six weeks of your arrival to avoid legal complications. I promise you, should you find conditions here not to your liking, I will be responsible for return tickets for you and the children to your point of origin.

My home is about four years old and is situated on my ranch on a promontory overlooking the Cimarron river and within sight of Black Mesa, the highest point in Oklahoma. It is a sparsely populated area of the State and Country.

The climate is temperate, with little snow or

rain. Temperatures in summer go over 100 degrees Fahrenheit regularly. That is about thirty degrees Celsius. It is arid country, but not a desert. I raise beef cattle and buffalo and a few cutting horses on about 3000 acres. I have several mineral leases and these provide me with an ample monthly income, regardless of my ranching operation. In fact, according to my accountant I am considered very comfortable financially. Once you are over here, I will open all my books for you and provide you with funds to cover our monthly household expenses. This will include funds to provide all of the children's needs also. It goes without saying, that I will be responsible for all your needs.

I own the ranch free and clear of any encumbrances. The same goes for the house and all vehicles. You will be provided a new SUV to use as you see fit. If you have a driver's license bring it and obtain an International Driver's License. At any rate, I will see to it that you will be able to drive and have a license.

Responsibility for the children's medical and educational expenses will be mine. I should think that I would want to adopt them once we are married, and they will be my heirs just as any future offspring. This includes a college education, if they so choose.

Now, to the house itself. As I said it is a relatively new structure, built of rose colored brick with Texas sandstone accents. It is just over 4000 square feet and is built to the most modern standards. It contains four bedrooms, three and a half bathrooms, a formal dining room and breakfast area, a library and great room as well as a modern kitchen and utility room.

There are ample closets and a large den and three garages. There is plenty of space for the children to play inside during inclement weather. Plus, their individual bedrooms are large enough to play in and to have a desk for school work. I do hope this satisfies your wishes as far as a home is concerned.

If you have any questions, just ask. I will try to answer all inquiries.

If it is agreeable with you, I should like to have you and the children here for the winter holiday season. Thanksgiving is the last Thursday in November and the Christmas season starts the next day. The children should have so much fun. I just hope this is not rushing you too much. Please let me know as soon as possible, so I can get started over here to make the arrangements for everything.

I should hate to have you all endure another cold Russian winter.

Please be so kind and send to me your exact sizes for clothing, plus your weight and height for both you and the children. I might want to purchase

14

some things for you and with that information at hand a friend of mine should be able to help me choose what might be needed.

Like you, I have lost my spouse. She died nearly twenty years ago. Unlike you, we had no children. We had wanted them dearly, but it never happened. So, your little ones will be very welcome here.

I really do not have any relatives. My grandparents raised me and have been gone many years now. My dad died in Korea when I was young and my mother left after that. I don't know what happened to her, but her folks were of Russian immigrant stock. I visited them a few times during summer break, but they too have passed on.

Please tell me the names and ages of your children. They look very young in the picture and how long have you been a widow? Tell me a little about yourself, should you decide to take my offer.

Forgive me for writing such a long letter. It might bore you, but if you should come, I think most of what I wrote might be of interest to you.

I hope to hear from you soon. More important I hope you have not changed your mind or that you have already accepted some other invitation.

With great anxiety and hope

Cliff Collins

Katja send this letter to Cliff, a few days after receiving his proposal. She could remember it word for word.

Dear Collins;

Thank you for your long letter. I received it several days ago, but had to find someone to help me decipher it. First of all, I have not received another serious offer. After quite some heavy thinking, and conversation with my friends, I have decided to accept your generous offer.

My three-year-old daughter Irina is excited about her Papi, as she started calling you the minute I showed her your picture. My five-year-old son Aleksandr is more skeptical. It is hard for him to think of leaving the only home he has known and all his friends. Sasha is old for his age, because for three years now he has been the man in my life.

Irina was born three and a half months after her father's death.

My husband Sergey, died from a combination of accidents. He was injured at his work site on the railway that connects our village to Yekaterinburg. He could not heal because of the exposure he suffered from the Chernobyl atomic accident. We did not know he was infected, or we would have seen to it, he took less dangerous work. Because two different agencies are responsible for his death, the authorities have not yet decided who is responsible for mine and the children's support. I have been expecting a determination for over three years now.

I too, work for the railroad on the maintenance of the line. It is extremely heavy work and dangerous. Because of the state of affairs in Russia, our pay checks have not been on time for a long time now. It is again six months outstanding. For these combined reasons, I find myself in deep financial straits. I am all but destitute. But I owe no one any money. My bills are current, but another two months will find me penniless. In Russia, you cannot owe money. No one will extend credit.

This is another reason, why I have decided to leave. I am worried over the lack of funds due me. I worry more about my children. What would happen to them if I was injured or killed on the job. We too have no relatives. Both of my parents are deceased and Sergey never found out what became of his parents and sister after the nuclear accident.

I know very little of my mother's family. She was born near Kiev and was sent out here to be secretary at the Internment camp. She died when I was twelve. Dad lived to be ninety-two and died only a few years ago. Dad had a brother who was engaged to be married in 1918. He was in St. Petersburg during the Revolution. Papa never found out what happened to his brother or parents or if Uncle Ivan married and had children.

We live in two attic rooms in the dacha that once belonged to my father's family high in the Ural Mountains on the Asian side of the range. For water, I must go down to the communal bathroom and bring it up in a bucket. We have a chamber pot which I empty twice daily. All waste has to be carried down three flights of stairs.

The dacha is a strong, sturdy dwelling, but no maintenance for over fifty years is telling. Although my rooms are small, I am more fortunate than a lot of people. I have a stove to warm the place and to cook our meals. Plus, the furniture are all heirlooms that were at the dacha in my grandfather's time. I perhaps have too many things.

The children stay with an old lady on the ground floor while I am working. Olga Kerchenova is a friend, who knew my father when he was a young man. She sees after the children without the constant indoctrination they would receive at a State-owned facility.

All of my friends and I help each other, when funds get short. It is the only way to survive.

We live in the village of Novorotskoye in Siberia, not far from the Arctic Circle. I suspect to come to America we would have to take the train to Yekaterinburg and from there take the weekly Trans-Siberian train to Moscow and from there fly to America. I know of no other International Airport to get me out, unless I would go to Tashkent and from there to India or to Tbilisi and from there to Turkey. I believe going to Moskva would be easier. I leave that up to you. There is no travel agent in this town for me to ask these questions.

As to our sizes: I am 1.52 m tall and weigh 47 Kilo. Rina is 68 cm tall and weighs 17.5 Kilo and Sacha is 85 cm tall and weighs 22.5 Kilo. As to American sizes I do not know and shoe sizes are different here too. But we all have serviceable foot wear.

I have no idea how much money I will need to pay for a hotel for one night in Moscow or for a bus fare to get us from the train station to the airport. I also do not know how much food costs on the train or what charges I might have on the airplane.

I promise to be frugal and give you back any money we don't need. I think 100 Rubles would be enough to reimburse my friends for small expenditures and about that same amount for daily lessons in English for one month. I hope that is not asking for too much. I have no idea what a Ruble is worth in Dollars.

I hope you find me not too demanding. Your

home sounds lovely and it seems impossible for one family to have so much space. Perhaps, I have not translated the dimensions properly.

I should think, we could be ready to leave here within two weeks of receiving your documents for travel. I will start working toward an end of November departure. I will quit my job and focus on learning more English.

I can send a telegram when I receive your travel documents, so you will know everything is in order. I hope this arrangement is satisfactory to you. It would be difficult for me to find a telephone to call you for final arrangements. Neither my friends nor I have one and the only public phone in town is accessible only during business hours. With the time difference between our locations, it would mean I wake you up during the middle of the night.

With greatest regards and best wishes, looking forward to our meeting I am

Katja

This was how it all had started, now it was time to finally leave. Katja thought to herself, as she once more looked around the rooms that had been her home, all her life. So, this was *It*, the beginning of the adventure, the end of this phase of her life.

For the last time, she would see these beloved, cramped, dark rooms. The rooms where she had lived her entire life, where she had been born, been a toddler, like Irina, her daughter, was now. The rooms where her mother had suffered and died. The rooms where she had become a young bride and where her devoted father had passed away. The rooms where she had become a mother and a widow. Rooms that had been used long ago as servant quarters, when the dacha was the hunting lodge of her ancestors, the counts Novorotsky.

The children were ready to go. They were dressed and sitting on their suitcases, backpacks strapped to their small frames. They were so tired. Little Irina had begged to sleep just a little longer and was asleep sitting upright, waiting for her mother to tell her it was time to go. The new warm Parka obscured her small body, her face hidden beneath the wool cap and hood and behind the big colorful muffler, her hands stuffed into warm insulated mittens.

Aleksandr too, was hidden beneath his new outerwear. Only he was awake and watching his mother intently. He was so scared, what would life be like, far away from here? He could not imagine. Would it be like "Walker Texas Ranger", with villains all about? With guns blazing everywhere? He liked to watch that show with his friend Sergey, on the television in his friend's rooms. His mother was in their sleeping room, the door open so he could see her. What was she doing in there? He hoped she would be changing her mind about leaving. He did not want to leave. He loved living here. They had always been here. They'd had enough food and the rooms were warm and cozy. Their friends were all here.

What if the man was a brute and beat his mother? What could he do? Oleg had said, he would have to protect his mother now. That he, almost six-year-old Aleksandr was now the man of the little family. But what could he do against a big, mean man? Aleksandr knew about mean men. The mother of his friend Sergey was always being beaten by her man, when he was drunk. And he was frequently drunk. Sergey and his sister Elena were happy when he was gone and often hid under the beds to escape his wrath. Oh, yes, he knew about mean men.

This man looked like a huge, mean monster in the picture he had sent them. Rina, that little fool, had called him her Papi from the first-time Mama had talked about him, when she had shown them his picture. Rina did not even know their Papa. She had not even been born then. Yet, she called this huge man her Papi. He, Sasha, had known Papa. Kind, gentle, dark haired Papa, with the blue eyes, that shone like jewels. Yes, that was their Papa, the one in the picture on Mama's dressing table.

Here Aleksandr paused in his thinking. He was so tired. If he could sleep just one little bit longer. When would be the next time he would be able to sleep in peace? He did not know, just that it would be long time hence. Then the thought of his father came back, but the face was blank. He could not remember what Papa looked like any more. That realization frightened him. He was just like Rina. How terrible to have forgotten what his Papa looked like. He had died such a long time ago. He, Aleksandr, had been smaller than Rina was now.

His mother came out of their sleeping room. She closed the door softly and shouldered her backpack. No, she had not changed her mind. Aleksandr was feeling forlorn and panicky.

Ekaterina Nikolayeva Novorotskaya slowly turned around in a circle. Her eyes were fastened on each object in the room. She was trying to fix every item into her memory; the writing desk under the window with her family's coat of arms carved into the center door, the painted cupboard that once stood in the dining room and displayed the specially made blue onion porcelain from the imperial china makers. The small table and chairs that once were used in the breakfast room of the dacha. The bookcases lining the walls of the little room filled with books her father had been able to retain. The two old easy chairs, now sadly in need of new fabric. All these pieces of furniture and the ones in their bedroom had belonged to the dacha and had been made for her ancestors and embellished with the family's coat of arms.

Now she was leaving all that was familiar behind in her quest for a more secure future. Was she doing the right thing? Should she have stayed here? Doubts assaulted her once again, and once again, she shook her head. No, there was no future here for her or her children. Just four weeks ago, she had again been penniless. The paycheck from the railroad had arrived six months late again, and now the remainder was outstanding five months again. She would have had to sell more of her precious heirlooms, if he had not send the money to her. No, resolutely, she adjusted her backpack. She was doing the right thing. One more sweep of the room. Yes, everything was in order, she had forgotten nothing. She patted her waist, where her money, passports and visas, as well as all the other important documents were hidden in a pouch beneath the bulky, padded overcoat she had been given. Now, the time had come to go.

Irina was still sleeping. Gently, Katja nudged the little girl.

"Come Rina, we must leave now." Instantly the little girl jumped up, and picked up the handle of her suitcase and started pulling the tightly packed red bag across the room.

"Little one, let your brother go first, like we practiced, careful, quietly, everyone is sleeping."

"Olga Kerchenova said she would be up and say good bye to us. She will be waiting downstairs." Sacha was sure.

24

"Perhaps, but it is late at night; everyone should be sleeping." With that she opened the door and picked up the handles of her two huge suitcases and wheeled them towards the stairs. The bare bulb lighting the hallway cast shadows everywhere, barely able to illuminate the stairs. She could hear Olga coming up.

"Katja, wait. Let me help you." The old woman came up panting, reaching for a suitcase.

"You help my little bird."

But no, Rina was a big girl now, and they had practiced yesterday how she was to walk down and hold onto the banister with one hand and pull her bag with the other. With a lot of noise and clatter, they all reached the front door. Katja was horrified, they might have wakened the whole house. No, they were all standing there, Sergey, his mother and sister, and the newest friend of Madame Bulin and her older daughter, Nikolay Levoto, his wife and their grandchild, who lived on the second floor. Everyone pressed in on them, hugged them and wished them farewell. Then she and the children were out the door.

The cold assaulted them the minute they stepped outside. It was a clear night, with stars sparkling above and so cold their breath froze instantly. A crackling, icy cold that numbed the exposed flesh in seconds. Katja was glad for the warm clothing they had received. She made sure the children had their hoods tightly over their heads and muffler and caps wrapped around their faces leaving only the eyes exposed.

It was then that she saw Oleg Mikhailovich with his transport sleigh and horses waiting for them in the street. The horses were stamping their feet and blowing huge streams of frost from their noses.

"Hurry, come, I'll take you. The horses must move." They heaved the heavy cases into the back of the transport sleigh and then clambered after them to sit on them while Oleg placed heavy fur blankets about their bodies. Katja was thankful they did not have to walk to the train station. A half hour in this cold might spell disaster. Walking in the heavy snow and cold would have had them all sweating and that was more dangerous than being just cold.

The horses pulled the sleigh effortlessly, and in just a few minutes, they arrived at the train station. A train was waiting at the platform. That train could not be theirs, for they were quite early. Oleg helped them out of the sleigh and then kissed the children good bye. He tried to press a few rubles into Katja's hand for a porter in Moscow and for tea on the train. Katja could not accept. She knew he'd go without warmth to give her the money.

"No Oleg, I have money. I should pay you for the ride on this cold night." She squeezed a few more rubles into his coat. With tears in his eyes, he left. The horses could not be left standing for long.

Suddenly, her friend Tatiana Bukhachev was there pressing a sack into her hand.

"Sandwiches and some fruit for the train."

"You sold it. How much?" There was no need to ask what she'd sold. The only thing of value that Tatiana possessed was a wonderfully warm silver fox coat. That coat was the last of Tatiana's possessions of any value, and she had threatened to sell that coat for a long time.

"Not enough."

"Here, go get it back." Katja handed her friend a small fortune. The sandwiches might come in handy after all. How much could tea and food be on the train? The station master was calling that the train was waiting for her. They were leaving a few minutes early for there was heavy snow on the way. The engineer wanted to be far down the track when the storm hit. Everyone was hugging her.

"Don't forget us. We love you. Please write." Tatiana and Olga were crying, and so was Katja.

"Don't sell my things just yet. If it does not work out, I was promised a ticket home and I have a little money. My paycheck from the railroad came just three days ago, with all the back pay." That was a lie,

27

but who would know? Olga promised. Katja gave her a few rubles too.

"Try to keep my things, please. I'll try to send for them." They had discussed what she would most like to have shipped. After giving every one of her precious few rubles, she was worried that she might not have enough money left to pay for food, a taxi and the hotel. She still had dollars, they would take them in Moscow, maybe?

Suddenly, they were alone in their train compartment. The engine started moving. Katja pressed her face against the window until the last shred of her friends and her small village had disappeared behind a hill.

Turning around, she found the children asleep on their seats. Her doubts assailed her again. Was she doing the right thing? Her friends had always been there for her. Now, she would be alone, without friends, without language even.

What if he did not like her, or she him? What if he did not like her children? What if it all was just too different? The "what ifs" kept coming uninterrupted while she lowered the children's berths and took off their coats, hats, mittens and mufflers.

Her mind was once again racing across well covered ground. Her friends had always been there for her; somehow, they'd all survived. She still had a few things to sell, and she had a job. She still could get off the train and return. But no, she had made the right choice.

Life in Russia for her was hopeless. Yes, she could survive for a little time longer, and then what? There was no hope for anything better. No hope for the children to go to a good school, to attend university. In the new Russia, one needed money, and she just did not have enough, and there was no chance of that situation to be ever any different.

Yes, her friends would help whenever they could. Just like now. What, heaven forbid, if something should happen to their children? Would they not soon resent the burden she and her children represented? Did she not see the relief on their faces when she gave them all a little money just now?

She wanted a bit of security for the children and herself. Mr. Collins represented that, a way of getting away from the numbing poverty. He offered that. He had responded to her desperate ad with generosity. He'd send her and the children tickets to fly to America and these suitcases and all these warm clothes. In the last of his two letters, he had asked her for her and the children's sizes, weight and height, and when the big box arrived, everything fit.

He had to be kind, sensitive and considerate. He'd filled the little purse, she now wore around her waist, with Rubles and Dollars and told her not to take much in the way of clothes, just enough for three days on the train and the day in Moscow and another on the plane.

They did not have more than that anyhow. In fact, she had to purchase a few items. He had told her not to bring any Rubles back with her. They were worthless anywhere else. Spend it, have a little fun on your last day in Russia. Yes, she had done the wise thing. Only time would prove that, but in her heart, she knew she was right.

She just sat there on the seat looking out of the window. All she saw was the night and darker shadows passing by. This was the last time she would ever see the stars over her own part of the world, clear and sparkling in the night sky. She had left the village where she had been born behind forever, the small village, on the eastern side of the Ural Mountains, in Siberia where she had lived for all of her thirty-seven years.

The time was now a little after 4:00 A.M. in her part of the world. She wondered what time it was now in Oklahoma. Was Mister Collins working his fields? Was it cold there too? Probably, she answered her own question. After all, it was almost December. She wondered how much snow there was on the ground in Oklahoma, USA. What was the name of the town, she'd forgotten, something City? Oh, well, she would remember later.

Mr. Collins had written that they did not live in town, but somewhere fifteen miles to the north and west of there. Quite near a river with a name that sounded something like Cinnamon. She had not been able to decipher his writing. Cinnamon, however, sounded nice to her. Sweet even, hot chocolate with a dash of cinnamon was a special treat.

The train was moving ever further away from home, away from all she had ever known. Katja closed her eyes for a second. God, she was so tired. There had been so much to do. She had a hard time to finish off all her business in such a short time: to decide which of her belongings to keep, what to sell, and what to give away.

The idea of the box had come to her, when she received the big box from Mister Collins containing the luggage and the winter coats. In the box, too, there was the little money pouch filled with dollars and rubles, more than she had ever had before. She felt immensely rich when she found the money. There also was a little camera and rolls and rolls of film, with the instruction to photograph everything she loved from every angle, to use up all the rolls and then place them in the magazines in which they arrived and bring them all to Oklahoma with her.

She had repacked the box with the things she wanted to take with her, but were too cumbersome to take along in her suitcases. Paintings of the dacha as the house once had been before the revolution, of her ancestors with Czar Aleksandr. A painting of the ancestral home in Russia near the Ukrainian border, south where the weather was warm. She had never seen it. Nor had she been to the family residence in St. Petersburg, where she hoped her uncle still lived.

She had packed the old Samovar with all of the remaining silver pieces with the family crest. The few pieces of imperial china she still possessed, remembrances of another time. There were two icons of good quality and the family picture album. The box was heavy, when she finished with it.

To send that box had cost her precious dollars to mail. What was left of the family jewelry resided in the pouch around her waist. She would wear all those gems when she left Russia, except for a couple of pieces, which she had secreted in the bottom of the samovar. They would have been too precious and too dangerous to sell.

Katja sat there resting, while her mind was busy with all the concerns she had, past present and future. The knock on the compartment door startled her. She was bewildered, did not know where she was. Sunlight was streaming in through the window, and the country side was rushing past. The children, are they safe? One look and she could see they were fast asleep. The knock came again, this time more urgently. Were they going to arrest her for trying to leave the country? The fear gave her cotton mouth.

She was unable to swallow. Cautiously Katja opened the door just a slit. A woman with a samovar on a cart offered tea.

"Breakfast is being served in the dining car 'till 10:30 A.M."

The relief was such that Katja almost asked the woman into her berth. How much would breakfast cost? She still had all those sandwiches Tatiana had sent.

"Oh, nothing for you dear. You paid all your meals in advance, see here. Did you forget?" The train worker showed Katja on the proffered tickets that all meals had been included. "So just wake the youngsters, and have a hearty breakfast down in the dining car. It's the next car over. Here now, Comrade, have your tea." The woman was big and garrulous and helpful.

Later, Katja might be able to get some information out of her, such as from which platform the train to Moscow was going to leave, and did it take a long time to get from where this train arrives to where she had to go?

The children were awake, when Katja stepped back into the compartment. Both had their noses glued to the window, watching Siberia rush away. They were on the way to Yekaterinburg, as

Sverdlovsk was now called again, and a meeting with the Trans-Siberian Railway there on its journey west to Moscow. Tonight, they would get on the express train to the city on the Moskva river and in two days, they should arrive in the capital of all the Russians.

This was the time for savoring a cup of tea. Later, she'd take the children to the dining car and they would have that hearty breakfast she was promised. They'd have lunch there too. Just before supper, it would be time to think about disembarking this train and wait for the other. There would be plenty of time to have supper in the station's restaurant before the Express train arrived.

The children were not bored that day. Aleksandr was still ambivalent about going to America. He would rather cope with the known reality. Irina found delight in each new adventure that her Papi had been so thoughtful to provide, as to make their journey so much fun. Had he, Sasha, ever eaten in a dining car? See how good her Papi was? The time dragged on. The children were at times bickering, as all children are wont to do at times. Their good humor always returned, just to watch what was going on outside.

"Mama, are there wolves in these woods?"

"I don't know. I would not be surprised if we saw some."

After that, each farm yard dog became a wolf, and a big black bear was around every corner. Katja tried to explain that the bears would be sleeping now until spring time. No matter, Irina saw them lurking in the distance.

The train stopped at regular intervals at stations of bigger towns. The children watched houses and schools and factories slide by their window. They pointed at other children playing in the snow or wash drying on clotheslines frozen stiff as boards. They giggled at the snowball fights going on in unnamed villages beside the track.

After a while an old man joined them in their compartment. He watched the children smiling. Irina asked him if he was going to Moscow, also. No, he was going only to Yekaterinburg. He was going to see his grandchild.

They all watched as the snow started falling again. First came only a few small flakes. Then, the snow grew heavier, until it was almost a blizzard. The engineer slowed the progress of the train to a crawl, but he did not stop. The train arrived later and later at each successive station. Katja was beginning to worry that they might miss the Moscow train. To keep the children entertained, their companion told them Russian fairy tales about the snow princess and the firebird.

As the train wound its way across the snow-covered countryside, Katja's thoughts once again returned to all her worries. Should she have stayed? Everywhere in Russia, there were such kind-hearted people, such as this old man keeping her children entranced with his tales.

For a while, she thought happy thoughts of staying with her friends. She could survive another year or two. Hopefully, by then, the government would have figured out a way to pay its workers regularly. Maybe she could have even found a better paying job. Yes, that was it. She should have stayed. By that time, too, the government would have made a decision about who had to pay her widows benefits and the children's benefits from their father. That additional income would make all the difference. That money would pay for the things they had to do without for the last three years.

The conductor came and knocked on the compartment door and informed all in a loud voice that their train would be arriving in Yekaterinburg a minimum of four hours late. They could all have more hot tea, but the dining room was closed, since there was no other food, because the expected time of arrival in Yekaterinburg had been prior to dinner time, and so no additional foods had been stocked. Katja watched as all color drained out of the old man's face.

"But I must have food at very regular intervals, so I can take my medication. Those are the doctor's instructions. I can die very quickly, if I don't follow orders. You must have a few little morsels in the kitchen. An old crust of bread should do."

"No, there is nothing. You should have brought something to keep you going. We cannot be responsible for your troubles." With that, the conductor slammed shut the compartment's door on her way to give her cheerful news to other hapless travelers.

The old man was trembling. Katja was afraid he would be unconscious within minutes.

"Don't worry so. You can eat with us. We have a sack of sandwiches and have not used any of them. Let me go and get some hot tea for us all, and then we shall eat."

When Katja returned minutes later, he was once again happily regaling her children with stories. They shared sandwiches and sausages and a piece of cheese and an apple, which their companion quartered with his little pocket knife. Afterwards, the children fell asleep and Katja was once again alone with her thoughts.

The kindness of her fellow Russian countrymen always surprised her. The ones that could least afford to help, did. But cruelty, too, was close to the surface, with officialdom to hide behind. Would she have been able to continue to contend with that?

What would happen if she could not get her benefits? Would she have to sell herself as so many did? How long or how often would she be able to do that? She was already in her late thirties. Younger, prettier women would always be available, for a price, she knew. What would happen if she contacted an illness? Where would she and the children be then?

Tatiana had said she was doing the same, but no, she was not. Otherwise every other married woman in the world was selling herself. No, Mr. Collins and she had a commitment for life. He seemed kind and caring, and she would do her best to be a good wife to him. Yes, she was doing the right thing. Had Mr. Collins not promised to care for her children, treat them as his own, see that they were healthy and educated?

No one in Russia had made such a promise. What would happen to her once she was no longer able to perform the hard labor on the railroad, that she had done in the past? Then, what was she going to do for an income? There was no question at all; she was doing the right thing.

Katja was interrupted in her thoughts by the old man. "So, tell me, where are you going with these children. You seem to be troubled and your son does not seem to want to go, but your daughter is happy?"

"We're going to America."

"So far, and so lucky. I've told my granddaughter to go, should she get the opportunity. She works for one of the petrol exploration companies as secretary. She has a good job, and she is paid every month. She wants me to stay with her and help her with her daughter, in exchange for living with her. My wife died a little while ago, and I just can't get along alone very well. I told Raja that she must get away from Russia, if she can. Of course, you must go. A chance for a better life comes along only once. You must take it. Do not listen to anyone but yourself. You must go." He was smiling at her, happy for her.

During their conversation, the train had picked up speed, and now they were traveling again at top velocity. A look out of the window confirmed that the snow had stopped. They were nearing a population center; lights were more numerous. They should soon be at their destination.

Katja gathered their things, then dressed the children and herself. The conductor came by and informed her that the train would arrive in Yekaterinburg in a few minutes. The Moscow train would wait for them so people could make their connections.

"You must hurry; they will wait only five minutes after our arrival. The train is on track one. We arrive on track three. You must hurry."

Katja herded the children to the door, said

good bye to their travel companion, and gave him the remainder of her sandwiches. She had no way to carry them. The long-practiced walk from one platform to the other would be useless now. That would take far too much time. The old man had the idea of strapping the smaller cases to the larger ones, making them ride piggy back. He even found some rope to bind them together. Now, Katja would only have to worry about little Irina being able to keep up and heaving the heavy suitcases up the stairs to the number one platform.

People were lining up by the exit doors as the train pulled into the station. Katja looked for a porter; there was none. No one was willing to work on this cold, late night. She was on her own. Suddenly, her old companion was at her side.

"You jump down. I'll hand you the children and then your luggage."

"Thank you," was all she had time to say, and then they were running for the stairs.

A voice behind her called out, "Comrade, wait, I'll help!"

That was the lady who had brought her tea all day. At the stairs, she caught up. "Give me the little girl and one set of luggage. I'm off for the night. I have a minute to help such a nice comrade."

Somewhere, the woman was stuck in the Soviet area, but that did not matter. Katja was grateful for the help. They reached the bottom of the stairs in no time. By the time, they got to the upstairs, they were both huffing and puffing. When they finally reached the train, Katja was hugging the woman with affection. She pressed several bills into the woman's hands, more grateful than she could express.

The conductor helped her and the children aboard and showed them to their compartment. Katja and her children were the last ones to reach the train, before it started rolling. They were on their way to Moscow, to the United States, to a better life.

The train ride to Moscow seemed never ending. All the more so, since they were delayed by snow for more than a day. The voyage was also boring and interesting at the same time, arduous and relaxing all at once, and surprisingly dirty. After the exertion of running for their connecting train, the children were ready to sleep. The proffered cups of hot chocolate, which the tea server brought, made them drop off even faster.

Katja sat over her glass of hot tea for a long time. Her mind kept conjuring all sorts of images. For a while, she indulged in happy thoughts about that perfect home she was going to have in Oklahoma. The one, where they would have their own kitchen and a bathroom to themselves and maybe even a bedroom for the children to share. Mr. Collins had told her about the house where he lived, but Katja thought he might just have exaggerated a bit, or his Russian was perhaps too imperfect. Her English also left a lot to be desired. She could not in her wildest dreams imagine such a house as he described. Still, anything would be better than the two five by six-meter attic rooms she had left behind at the dacha.

Mr. Clifford Collins could not be anything but wonderful. Had he not sent a picture of himself to her. Did he not look so handsome? Had he not been so thoughtful in his dealings with her? She drifted into slumber. But when the train stopped at one of the stations, she jerked awake.

Once the train got going again, she watched the landscape for a long time. There was a heavy coat of snow covering everything like a huge, white, down blanket. The moon reflected on the shiny frozen crust. Lakes shimmered like mirrors in the distance. The mountains receded and made way for the big, flat plains.

Katja thought about the difference of her trip, compared with the trip her father had taken to the hunting lodge in the Ural Mountains, when it seemed that things could not get any worse in early winter of 1916/17. She had been told the whole story numerous times. Now it was a new century, 2001. Papa had lived a long life and had seen the fall of communism. He had outlived his wife, who had been younger than he, by many years. He had known Sergey, her husband, but not his grandchildren. She had been expecting Aleksandr, when Papa had passed. He had regretted not getting to know that child. That had been one of the last things he had told her, before losing consciousness, before the end.

It had been such an arduous adventure for a child, and her father had been little more than a child, a few months past his fourteenth birthday. That had been such a dangerous voyage. It had taken the boy several months to arrive at the dacha, evading the marauding serfs.

His parents, her grandparents, had packed the troika with family heirlooms and documents, pictures and paintings, warm clothes and blankets, food for him and his horses and his servant, until they were unable to stuff another item into the sled for the journey. There were maps with the route and alternates marked, a gun for hunting and one for defense. One of the family's trusted serfs was to go with the boy. He was an older man, whom her father had known since his infancy. The troika was magnificent, encrusted with gold leaf ornamentation and the family crest on the doors. The horses were spirited and pranced with excitement.

Once they left his parent's estate, Igor, the servant, took over the reins, and her Father had settled comfortably into the cushions. They came through towns and villages on their way to the dacha. Many of the farms were without anyone there. Igor had stopped several times, to see if they could purchase food, or just to see where everyone was. The servants had left.

In the towns, there were marauding serfs everywhere, looting and pilfering. The Bolsheviks were arresting people. That was scary! Her father had remained hidden in his seat. He could not understand what was happening. He and his family had always been fair to their serfs and servants. Well, maybe not Ivan, his older brother. But he and Mother and Father had never mistreated them. He could not understand what the unrest was all about. Surely, things would settle down; they always did.

Mother had brought the family's big troika down from St. Petersburg, when she had returned in the spring from a season of balls and presentations at court. Ivan had been there with her, but he had remained in St. Petersburg. He was a captain in the Czar's own regiment, and he had wanted to remain close to the princess to which he was engaged.

He, Nikolay, her father, together with her grandfather, Count Petr Petrovitch Novorotsky had been at the hunting lodge, to which the boy was now returning. They had been there all last winter. He knew, as second son, he could not inherit the title and all that went with it. Father knew, he would have to be a soldier or a cleric or some sort of professional.

His father would purchase him a commission, if he so wished, or set him up in a nice church or send him to school, if he so desired.

Nikolay, her father, however had no desire to do so. He loved the earth, was happiest, when he was digging in her soft, black soil. He had been planting flowers and vegetables for as long as he could remember. His mother had encouraged his passion and had ordered the gardener to provide Nikolay with a small plot. Instead of building sand castles as a youngster, he had planted.

As he grew older, he had worked with the serfs in the fields. He had reaped the grain and sowed it, furrowed it and studied how the crop was progressing. He had formulated his own ideas of what was important to a good crop, things he could do to improve the yield. He planted the potatoes and watched with fascination as the green tops appeared with the little white flowers that turned into green fruit. He knew how to use the scythe and cut hay.

He had the know-how to care for horses, cattle and pigs. At six, he had taken over the care of the estate's hens, and by the time he was twelve years old, he was able to make the decisions required to take care of the estate. In fact, his understanding had irked the foreman, but his father had instantly noticed, that his estate was far more productive than what had been before his young son took charge.

Nikolay knew his only option for providing him with a reasonable income in his lifetime lay in his ability to manage all of his father's and brother's estates. For that reason, he had been sent to the hunting lodge to bide his time, while the political unrest sorted itself out. While there, he might as well make the little place a little more productive. The money he saved his father there, would be part of his own stipend.

Katja's father and his servant Igor traveled all that day without finding anyone at a hostel, and so they decided, rather wisely, to sleep in some woods. Igor pulled the big sleigh off a road and hid in the woods. They ate what food they had and made tea from snow they scooped up. Nikolay slept in the troika, and Igor had bundled up under it. And so, they traveled for several days.

The crowds became ever more unruly and started throwing eggs and rotten tomatoes at the troika. Some even packed rocks into their snow balls. They crossed on a ferry over the Dnieper amidst hostile passengers. Igor became frightened, and for a while, Nikolay, her father, tended to the reins with the servant hiding in the coach.

Things did not get better. That night, they were camped not far from a hamlet. Igor refused to make a fire to heat water for some tea. He was muttering a lot to himself. The next morning, he was gone. It had snowed during the night. All tracks had been obliterated. When Nicolay woke, he could hear nothing. He called out to Igor, but there was no answer. Katja's father had thought the servant had gone to relieve himself, and later, he thought perhaps he'd gone to the hamlet for some hot food.

When after two hours, there was still no sign of the servant returning, Nikolay had faced that problem squarely. He roused himself, fed his horses, and while they were feeding, he made a small fire, then made some tea and found some left over dark bread and a hunk of cheese. After that, he had no trouble hitching his sleigh.

While having his breakfast, the boy had mulled over his options. He could not go back home. His father had given him strict orders not to return under any circumstances. He was to go to the dacha in the Ural Mountains on the Asian side. He was told to stay there until his father, mother or brother came to fetch him.

He had no place in St. Petersburg. The rioting was worse there than in the country. Going to the dacha in the Crimea was an option. All the nobility gathered along the shores of the Black Sea in summer. Perhaps he could hide out there, till the country settled down again. Only his parents would not know where to find him.

There was nothing for it. He had to go to the hunting lodge. It became quite clear to him; he could not go as he was. The rotten tomatoes, eggs and stones had delivered their message. He had to get rid of his troika and disguise himself as a laborer or peasant.

Nikolay traveled that day the most remote routes he could find. Towards late afternoon he found a deserted estate. Here, he should be able to make some alterations to his sled, or perhaps find another. Carefully, he pulled into a large barn and set out to explore the surroundings.

The estate was lifeless, save for four magnificent Belgian draft horses. They were in bad shape, hungry and thirsty and dirty. First things first, he took care of all the horses, his and the Belgians. After that he set out in search of lumber and paint and perhaps another sleigh.

Nikolay worked quickly and thoroughly. He found everything he needed to change his stately troika into a transport sleigh, and for changing himself from a noble boy into a young peasant. There was old clothing in the style the peasants wore, he took them. He found ugly green paint in a bucket. It seemed to him the workers had mixed together several colors and came up with this putrid green. He painted the entire troika with that awful paint. He hoped his father would forgive him, but he had to get rid of all the trappings of privilege and stature. The rioting masses would lynch him.

At first, he attempted to take off the wood

ornamentation but realized quickly that they lent structural support to the sides of the sleigh. It took him till late that night to cover all that beautiful, shiny, black lacquer. The boy was so tired; he fell asleep in the barn without food.

Katja remembered that her father had spent most of a week at that deserted estate. At the end of that time, his troika was unrecognizable. He too had changed from the young noble boy on a journey to the family's hunting lodge, to Nikolay Strachens, an eighteen-year-old Bolshevik on his way to the Urals to help with the revolutionary effort there. He had made himself papers to authorize his travel. Papers, that would pass muster, for he could read and write, but most of the rabble could not.

When his sleigh finally left that estate, the troika was a transport sled, with a roof rack full of hay, the cab full of grain and the wonderful velvet seats covered by burlap sacks. The sled was pulled by four Belgian draft horses led by his stallion. The two mares were tied to the rear, to be walked and exchanged, when one of the other horses needed a bit of rest. Making the changes to the sleigh that allowed him to have five horses pulling, rather than three, had been the most difficult change he had accomplished to affect to the sleigh.

Katja finally fell asleep sitting up, dreaming of her father's trip to Siberia and mixing it all up with her own trip out of Siberia. There was a monstrous man banging with something on her door. Katja woke with a start. It was still dark. The banging was somewhere to the rear of her coach, not at all on her door. The train was adding several wagons in the rear. It was nothing to be concerned about. She finally undressed somewhat and lay down on her bunk. This time, she fell asleep dreamless. When she woke, there was muted daylight. She could hear voices on their way to the dining car. Sasha and Rina were waking, too. It was time to begin the day.

The world outside her window was once again white. It was snowing again. It would be nice to have something to take her mind off her worries and off her wandering thoughts. A book or magazine would be a welcome diversion. Katja had neglected to bring anything along to read.

Once her children were fully awake, she cleaned and dressed them, and they made their way to the dining car. Several passengers were there already. Katja found herself seated next to a family with three children. They looked to be prosperous. Everyone was dressed in stylish western clothes. The mother looked absolutely stunning in her chic pantsuit. She seemed to have just stepped out of a beauty salon. Katja was feeling frumpy and jealous. Hairdos and make up had been pushed to the back burner since she had become a widow, and funds had been so scarce.

Those were luxuries she happily had done

without. Food for the children was so much more important than her appearance. It had been a long time since she used up the last bit of lipstick, and her hair had been cut most recently by her friend Tatiana. She usually wore it smoothed back in a bun at the nape of her neck, a la ballerina. By now the natural curl in it had probably escaped the constrains of the ribbon and stood in a fuzzy mess all over her head.

The style had been pleasing, if she could have kept all the hair contained. She had almost black hair and the wide, prominent cheek bones of her Slavic ancestors. Her build, however, was very petite, not at all like the Slavs. She must have taken after her paternal grandmother, who had been tiny and willowy and had studied to be a dancer with the Imperial Ballet Company. Grandfather had seen her on her one performance as prima ballerina and married her right away.

Now, Katja looked at her neighbor and felt inferior and dowdy. What would Mr. Collins think of her? Would he find her unattractive or dirty, or neglectful or worse? Would she have time in Moscow to get her hair done? Buy some lipstick? What would she do with the children while she was being fussed over? Her thoughts were interrupted by her precocious little daughter.

The irrepressible Irina was already talking to the smaller of the two girls, inviting her to play in their compartment. Only after the little girl had enthusiastically agreed to the plan did Rina think to ask her mother for permission. Of course, permission was given.

While everyone waited to be served, introductions were made. It turned out the family were Westerners, from England. They were returning there now, after a year's service with British Petroleum in Siberia. The Martin family would be staying in Moscow for several days visiting the sites, and then travel to St. Petersburg for a few days there to see the Winter Palace and the Hermitage, before returning to London. They were Nigel and Deena the parents, and nine-year-old Heather, seven-year-old Morgan and three-year-old Parker.

After breakfast, Deena Martin brought her brood over. She also brought several American Magazines.

"I hope you don't mind me joining the fun. Nigel needs to do some work on his laptop, and I always annoy him when he is working. I brought some things along to read. Hope I'm not a bother."

"Oh, I'd love it. I wanted to get out in Perm and find something to read, but I think, I slept through that stop. I'd love to visit.

"Na, you didn't. This train is running once again late. It's been that way most of this trip."

"Come have a seat. How long have you been traveling?"

"This is our fourth day on this train, and before that, we were for most of a day on one of the feeder trains. Travel in Siberia in winter is not much fun."

"It isn't fun in summer either, believe me. Then you're plagued by mosquitoes and mud, with the tracks sinking down to the perma-frost. I should know, I worked on the tracks for years."

"You? Tiny you? Don't they have enough big, fat men to do such jobs?" Deena was incredulous. "Why were they making you do such a job? Where you in exile or some such thing? Are you now going back to Russia?"

"No." Katja smiled. Could she tell this young woman her story? Or even part of it? What harm would it do? "I wasn't exiled or being punished. I just was born in Siberia, in the same village where I left from yesterday. Actually, I lived and was born in the house that was my father's family's hunting dacha. My children and I occupied the two attic rooms. No, I'm going to America to be married."

"You are? How wonderful, congratulations! Where in the States are you going? We lived in Texas a few years ago, for a little while."

"To Oklahoma."

"Where in Oklahoma? that's a fairly good sized State. What town are you going to Oklahoma City, Tulsa?

Deena was intrigued. In her years in the States, she had traveled quite a bit with her husband.

"No, neither one of those, although the town, too, has the name 'City' behind it. Mr. Collins wrote that it is a very small town, and he lives several kilometers from it, near a river called something like *Cinnamon*."

"The Cimarron runs through a large part of Oklahoma from west to east."

"How do you say that? *Cirramon*?" Katja was almost stuttering. She could not bring her tongue around to pronounce it properly.

"Cimarron, try it. Cima-rron, once again Cimarron." Both women giggled.

Heather had picked up on the conversation. Now she asked Aleksandr, "You're going to America? Want me to teach you English? Do you know any yet? You might want to know a few words so you can play with other children. I had to learn Russian before we came here last year. I had a tutor, who came to our house in London every day."

"What is English? Don't they talk like us in America? Everyone knows how to speak Russian." Sasha was definite. Didn't *Walker* speak Russian on his TV show from Texas? He wanted to play, not think about living far away. He did not even want to go. Now, he learned, that he'd have to learn to speak differently. He had not bargained for that.

"Every country speaks differently. Few people outside of Russia know Russian, but most folks know a little English, even here in Russia. English is spoken by a number of countries. England, of course, where we live, and America, where you are going to live, and Canada and Australia, and a bunch more that I don't know about yet. Mom and Dad learned Russian mostly after we got here."

"Does my Papi speak that English, Mama?"

"Yes, dear."

"Does he know Russian?"

"A little bit, Irina. His grandparents were Russian, but he thinks he is not so good at it, since it is the old way of talking, and so much English has found its way into his Russian. I know a little English. Remember, I went to Dimitri Gregorsky to have him teach me some the last few weeks?"

"Well, then I want to learn this English. I want to tell my Papi how happy I am that he let us come live with him."

"That is good, Rina, and thank Heather for teaching you. Sasha, you might need to know a few words too, so you can speak with Mr. Collins and can tell him thank you, or please, and that you need to use the bathroom or that you're hungry or thirsty. I think that might come in handy. Don't you think so, too?"

He could see the reason for those words. Practical Sasha consented to the lesson grudgingly. There was a lively discussion going on between the children. Irina asking for sentences she thought she might need to know and, Aleksandr reluctantly asked for words he thought important.

Heather was a good little teacher. She told them the meaning of a word, then pronounced slowly, had Sasha and Rina repeat it several times. Then, she moved on to another word. After having learned four or five new words, she always recapped the words they had previously learned. She stuck with the basic nouns and then slowly added verbs. When lunch time arrived, the children's faces were glowing. They had learned many words.

The women were talking quietly, so not to disturb the children. Katja had so many questions to ask about America. She had not known anyone who had ever been there. She was smart enough to know, the old party line, that they had been fed in school, would have been mostly lies and propaganda. So, here she had a chance to ask questions and have them answered by somebody who would know. Deena was happy to reply.

"Mrs. Martin, do you think, I was too demanding when I asked that we have our own bathroom, kitchen and a bedroom for the children to share besides our own? I've read that this is not uncommon in the West. I want a little better for the children than what I ever would be able to provide here."

Deena Martin laughed. "You most likely will have at least a bedroom for each of the children and a bath for them to share. You will also have a bath for yourselves. I do not know any American woman who shares her kitchen with another family. Don't worry, you did not ask for too much."

"Mr. Collins said in his letter, that his house has four bedrooms, three and one half bathrooms, a large kitchen, something he calls a *utity* room, a dining room and living room and what he calls an office, a den. What is that? And a breakfast room. Surely, they do not have a room to eat only breakfast in? He said the children would each have a bedroom, and we'd have a big bedroom and a big walk in closet. I think maybe he made things sound a little better than they are. I cannot imagine such a house. Only someone very rich would have something like that in Russia. Maybe someone in the Central Committee."

"No, Dear, I think he said exactly what he has. A four bedroom, three and one half bathroom house is not uncommon. The additional rooms he mentions are also common in a house of that size. Even very small houses have more than one bathroom and several bedrooms. Here, let me show you."

Heads bend over some magazines, and Deena explained the usage of several rooms, how they might be furnished and what the women did who lived in these houses. The utility rooms and master closet rooms where unbelievable to Katja. When Deena showed pictures of kitchens and master baths, Katja thought her new friend was putting her on. Only in movies could such luxury be expected.

The talk turned to other things, children, cooking, housekeeping, what you would expect women to talk about. There were other words though, that had been part of the letter Mr. Collins had sent, and their meaning was still a mystery to Katja.

"Deena, please help me understand something Mr. Collins wrote. He is talking of where his home is. First, he calls something that is his a 'ranch', then he said it is in something called a potholder? What does it mean?"

"Well, a ranch is a big farm that does not grow crops for the most part but raises cattle and maybe horses. I think, he meant to say a panhandle. Is that the word he used?"

"Yes, that's it."

"The State of Oklahoma looks on a map something like a sauce pan. The panhandle is a long narrow strip of land that extends west from the main part of the State. Did you say earlier that the town has the word 'City' attached to it?"

"Yes."

"Is it Boise City? Does that sound familiar? The Cimarron River is not far from there."

"Mr. Collins wrote that his ranch is in this panhandle fifteen kilometers north-west of this city and on that *Cimanon* river. He also wrote that he has several thousand acres. Is that possible? The State allows one person to own so much land?"

"Oh, sure. Especially in that part of the State. By the way, what is Mr. Collins full name? I seem to remember someone by that name, that we knew, when we lived in Amarillo."

"Clifford Collins. I don't know his patronym. He did not write that."

"Morgan, darling, go get your daddy. I want to ask him something."

"Mama, he is going to be mad if I interrupt him while working. I don't want to get into trouble."

"Morgan, go. Or you'll be in trouble with me."

Nigel Martin came into the room with a frown on his face.

"Deena, I'm in the midst of transmitting. What do you want?"

"Oh, darling, I think you'll like this. I'm quite sure. Don't we know someone in Oklahoma by the name of Clifford Collins? There is a memory somewhere, but I can't puzzle it out." She was grinning impishly.

Her husband tried to look stern but a mischievous grin played at the corners of his mouth.

"Deena surely you've not forgotten Uncle Cliffy? Why?"

"Katja, is going to live with him. They're getting married. They're on their way to Dallas where he will pick them up."

"So, he finally did it. I'll be. Lucky you, Katja, and lucky children." Katja blushed. There was a kind of pandemonium in the train compartment.

"You know, guys, it's time for lunch. I'm starving, let's go." Mister Martin shepherded his children out in to the corridor.

"Come along then, Katja. We have so much to talk about. I can't believe Uncle Cliffy is your fiancé. Who would have thought it?" Nigel Martin was chuckling to himself and mumbling into his beard. "That old bugger. He's finally done it. And what a looker he found. Have to give it to the old fart."

"Katja, did you say you had a picture of Mr. Collins? I'd like to look at it. We should be able to recognize him. If he is who we think it is, you found yourself a very nice man. There are many who'll be very jealous." Deena Martin chuckled too.

"I do, but his face is hard to see because of…" and here Deena joined in.

"The big hat," Nigel continued the thought and said to Katja.

"Stetson hat. It sure sounds like our Cliffy, but then most ranchers in America wear those ten gallon hats."

"Is that what they are called? You see them on TV."

Actually, they are Stetsons mostly, or Resitol hats. They're good, though. In the heat, they keep the face shaded and the sun out of your eyes, and in winter they keep you warm. The sun is still out most winter days. Those hats keep you from squinting all the time. But Uncle Cliffy wears them for another reason. He's almost bald. Just has a thin band of hair above the ears and in the back. With his big chapeau covering most of his scalp, he looks like he has a full head of hair. We kept laughing, that he wears the hat to bed. Only changes from straw in summer to felt in winter. I had to make him take it off inside the house." They all laughed.

The journey was continued by all in good spirits. They laughed and giggled as stories of Uncle Cliffy were related. Katja learned an enormous amount of what she could expect, how things were so different in the States. Most of what she was being told seemed so unimaginable to her.

The children studied English voluntarily and made quite some progress. The wondrous things Heather and Morgan told about made Rina quiver with anticipation. Sasha seemed to lose some of his fears and looked forward to new adventures. The days passed quickly, uninterrupted by the pristine white world outside their compartments.

Chapter Two

n Oklahoma, Cliff Collins was calling it a day. He had ridden fence most of it and found no significant breaks. He was tired, his back hurt, and his eyes stung from the light sand in the air, the strong, dry wind and from squinting all day. The sun had been relentless. His throat was so dry, he could not swallow anymore. He was dusty and sweaty. He needed a shower and a hot mug of java. Starbucks would hit the spot right now.

Only there were no Starbucks in Boise City, and the coffee at the Cafe in town would by now be mud. He shook himself. It would be another mug of Nescafe with perhaps a shot of Irish flavored International Coffee Creamer. Yep, that'd be it. Maybe after cleaning up, he could head over to Don and Donna's house and scrounge another meal. God, he was so tired of endless *Hamburger Helper* and tuna casserole or franks and beans and mac and cheese. Why had he never learned to cook a decent meal? He should have started something in the crock pot before he left for the range this morning. He'd have a hot meal waiting now. Yeah, right, he thought, it would probably be mush by now.

He swung out of the saddle, took the horse up to the barn, got the saddle and tack off, put a rug over the steaming sides of his mount and gave the beast a few handfuls of sweet feed. While the horse munched, Cliff rubbed him dry. Afterward, he turned the roan out into the pasture, put the saddle up and his tools and then trudged over to the house.

Just inside the back door, he pulled his old boots off. On his way to the bathroom, he filled the kettle with water for coffee. He started the water in the shower, and while it warmed, he stripped. As the hot steam from the shower filled his nostrils, he began to breath comfortably again. He let the water pummel his aching back. Life surged again into muscles. Still in his robe, he scooped up his dirty clothes and stuffed all of them into the washer. He wondered how come Don's white T-shirts stayed so white until they fell apart. Was that a secret only women knew how to do?

The kettle had long ago started to whistle. Now, he poured the hot water into a mug and added coffee crystals, sugar and creamer till the concoction resembled a cup of coffee. Not good, but passable. He slurped the first sip on his way back to his bedroom and there fell gratefully into his recliner. He relaxed, sipped his coffee. His eyes wandered around the room.

Just a few more days and then his life would change forever. Was he ready? Was he willing to share his life? Was he ready to share his home with a stranger? Was he ready for little kids to run screaming though his house? A big, old, white, fluffy cat came padding up to him and started rubbing herself along his chair.

"Princess, have you had a tough day? Have any little rodents tried to invade your territory? Have you had enough kibbles? The water is still dripping in the bathroom, if you need a drink."

"Wrau, mrau au," was her contribution to the conversation. She jumped into his lap and started kneading on his chest.

"Sweets, keep the sabers sheathed, or you will fly through the air again. Settle down." The cat evidently understood the remark about flying and instantly stopped digging her claws into her master's chest. He thought for a while,

"Where is Snow today? Have you seen him? He was with me this morning. After we left the cattle behind, I lost track of him."

"Wrau," came the replay.

"Princess, I wish you would speak human. I can't understand cat."

Cliff reached for the patio door, opened it, whistled and just a few seconds later a huge, white streak slammed against the door. Cliff stretched his hand out again and opened the door. The dog came in panting.

"Is everything okay in your department? No coyotes hanging around? Had a good day chasing vermin?" The dog settled himself with his head resting on Cliff's feet. A heavy sigh escaped as he settled in for a good snooze.

"Hey, guys, don't get so comfortable. I've got to pick up around here, and then I have to think about something to eat. A can of soup would be okay; don't you think, Snow? Maybe a sandwich? And for dessert, we could have a bowl of Sugar Pops? Naw, sounds like heck. Maybe Donna made enough goulash for me too? Maybe I'd better put some clothes on and get going. What do you guys think?" A heavy tail slapped the floor, and Princess started purring.

"I don't know how I am going to handle a human response to my trivial conversation. Do I even know how to talk to a person anymore? What if she is a weird kind of person? What if her kids are hellions? How am I going to handle sharing my bathroom? What if she snores? What if my animals don't like her or the kids?

Critters, is she going to understand that I talk to you all the time? I know it's a lonely person's defense. Will she understand? What if I don't like her? What if she is a slob? What if she is ugly? Hell, Cliff, you ain't no prize either. Cliff get up, get going. Hanging around here is going to drive you nuts. Talk to Donna, see what you still have to get and get a move on."

Resolutely, Cliff got up, dressed and then fed his pets. Snowball saw him put on his good jeans, a clean shirt and jumped around like a pup. The dog knew he would go along for a ride.

Sheriff Don Brewer and his wife Donna had been Cliff Collins' friends since they had been in grade school. In high school, they, along with his Mary, had been a foursome. They had double dated and then all gone off together to college. Cliff to Stillwater to study animal husbandry at the A&M college, now Oklahoma State University, Don to the University of Oklahoma in Norman, to study law.

The girls had both gone to Canyon, Texas to study at North Texas State, to become teachers. They had roomed together and been best of friends then, Donna and his Mary. No one in town had thought it odd, when they had married in a double wedding. Soon babies arrived at the Brewers house. They arrived at regular intervals, all six of them. Donna had joked that she needed to move out of the bedroom, so she could have a break from having kids.

He and Mary had wanted children, too. Half the time, Donna's brood spent in Mary's kitchen. Mary had ached for her own, but year after year, they had waited and hoped, for naught. Then, one day, Mary finally announced, crying with joy, that it finally had happened, they were expecting! Oh, they had been so happy. Doc had told her to take it easy. after all, she was almost thirty. And so, she had. Cliff had hired Inez Garza to take care of the heavy housework; then, to do all of the housework, as Mary was having more and more of a hard time.

By the time, Mary was six months along, she'd taken to her bed. Then, one day, not long after that, Inez had come screaming out to the barn, Mary had taken a bad turn. They called the doctor, who sent the helicopter, and they'd taken her by Medivac to North Texas Baptist Hospital in Amarillo. He'd followed along in the truck, but it was no good. When he got to the hospital, it was all over and his sweet Mary was gone. The baby never had a chance. He drove home a broken man. Don and Donna were by his side, when they put the two pitiful coffins into the soil.

That was oh-so-many years ago. He'd been alone ever since. For a long time, he could not date; he had no desire to. The thought of it felt like he was betraying Mary. When he finally had snapped out of his sorrow, the world had changed. He was an old albatross that did not fit in anymore. Donna tried to set him up with blind dates until she ran out of candidates.

As the opportunities to date faded away, he had spent his energies on other matters. Don had wanted to run for sheriff when the old one quit. Cliff supported his old friend and helped with the campaign. Don won, and when a short time later, the County Commissioner slot became available, he, Cliff, had run for it. He had prospered in every way. Now, he was quite comfortable and alone, forced to talk to his pets and imagine their answers.

Don and Donna, too, had their heartbreaks. The children grew up and moved away. There was so little opportunity for them here, and so they moved and made good lives for themselves and their families in Houston and Dallas, in Phoenix and Oklahoma City, in Atlanta and Las Vegas. Donna and Don grieved after their children; they missed them. They wanted to be part of the grandchildren's lives. They did not even know little Donnie, who was now almost six years old.

They too were alone, but they had each other to talk to in the shower and in the morning over their cups of coffee. They had each other to scratch that impossible-to-reach spot in the middle of the back. Donna had Don to smooth on lotion and bring a cup of tea in the evening after a long day. Clifford longed for that kind of intimacy, the kind that showed him someone cared, no matter what. Passion would be nice, but not necessary. What was necessary were the little things, the laughter and the sadness, that binds.

Cliff was mulling all this over, when he was on his way to his friends' home.

"Hi. Stranger, come in, have you eaten? I made an extra chicken fried steak, and there are mashed potatoes and gravy and beans." He almost cried, he was so overcome with gratitude. Donna filled a plate for him and Don moved some paperwork to make a space for him at the kitchen table.

How had he ever wound up in this spot? It had been a long journey. How had he come to this place, where he had to order a bride by mail? Why had he done that? Was he so undesirable?

"So, Cliffy, have you heard from Russia?"

"Not a word, Donna."

"When are they supposed to leave?"

"Yesterday morning, real early."

"And they never called?" Don was surprised.

"No, but she wrote in her last letter that she doesn't know anyone who has a phone at home. She had said that if she needed to talk to me, she'd have to find a private phone, because of the time difference. The Post Office would be closed during the night, which is our day time."

"So, when are they supposed to be here?

"Tuesday."

"What are you gon'na do?"

"Go down to Dallas and hope she comes. By the way, can you guys think of anything I ought to get for them, before they get here?"

Donna thought hard. "Maybe some toys for the kids and maybe a dictionary. I don't know, but you might like to get something for the kids to keep them from getting bored on the drive home."

"You got them some booster seats, right?" Don inquired.

"Don," Donna interrupted, "They're not babies anymore. That boy is going on six and the little girl is three. They don't need no baby seats, no more."

"Well, maybe not the boy, but that little girl

surely needs a booster seat. I don't mean those infant seats, you know, just a little booster, that they're supposed to have 'till they're about fifty pounds. Sets them a little higher and makes the seatbelt fit them better. I had Henry all day at the Walmart checkin' that the kids had the right seats, and they're installed proper-like."

"No, I haven't got anything like that. Do I have to have them?"

"I would. Don't know how strict those troopers are down in Texas, but the law is that you have them."

"Where do I get them? Any special type?"

"I guess Walmart or K-Mart or even Target or a kid's store. Don't get the baby seats. They're too big for that, but booster seats. They cost less too. Pick them up on your way or in Dallas."

"I'd better make a note of that. I guess I can pick them up at the Mall in Dallas. I was going to get some light clothes too, for them all. I bet, she has them kids bundled up like in Siberia, and Dallas can be pretty warm in December."

"And while you're thinking of buying stuff, pick her up a bunch of flowers."

"Why? We're staying in a motel for a couple

of days. They'd be all wilted by the time we got home."

"Flowers never hurt, right, Donna? She's a woman. Women love flowers, and they do have water glasses in hotels. Or are you planning on taking them to the no tell motel? You can always get her a vase at the Walmart." Don was chiding, but Donna nodded her head earnestly.

"Flowers would be good Cliff; roses would be the best. Remember, Mary loved them for any occasion. You want some more taters and gravy? Leave a little space for dessert. I'll let you guys take me to the Dairy Queen."

"Now, guys, you all have me spending money like I was Mr. Moneybags." He was kidding; he knew his friends were right about the flowers. Mary had always melted when he handed her a bunch.

"Cliffy, don't be a cheapskate now. That last well of yours, out on your back forty, has been pumping up solid gold all these years. Spend a little of it. If you want to impress that girl a bit, it's the thing to do."

"That's sure good food Donna. Can't wait for Katja to come. To have supper waiting when I get in from riding fence all day, is all I ever want. Dessert's on me. Let's go."

Later that same evening, as Cliff was leaving his friend's house, he hugged Donna and whispered, "Thanks for reminding me. Don't forget to make that list of things you want from town." But it was Don who asked if he could find him a nice white, lacy blouse for Donna's Christmas.

"When are you leaving for Dallas?"

"Monday morning, after chores."

"You might want to leave a little earlier than that. Dallas is a mighty long drive from here. Leave on Sunday; that way, you have time to do the shopping and scout out the place," Don advised.

"Want us to come over to feed Snowball and Princess?"

"No, thanks, though, Donna, Inez is going to do that and clean house really good."

That night, he dreamed of being rejected all over again. He had been thinking of the young woman he had taken out years ago. Over their steaks, he had asked her if she wanted to come out to the ranch and spend the day.

"No," had been the answer. "If you intend to let this relationship grow into something more than just the occasional dinner out, then you had better get rid of that ranch you're so proud of. I'm not under any circumstances going to bury myself in the middle of nowhere. If you want to be with me, then you had better plan on moving to Dallas or Houston, or any big town where there is fun to be had and something to do. I'm going to blow this town, the first chance I get."

Cliff was so stunned, he sat there for a minute with his mouth open. Then he had risen, called the waiter, paid him and had the maître d' call a taxi for her. He had left and gone home, alone and bewildered and dejected. After that, he had given up dating. That had been years ago.

As always, he woke up from this dream. He let his mind wander, in an effort to return to sleep.

The idea of finding someone from outside the country had slowly jelled. It had really taken on form, when he had learned that one of his fellow Commissioners had sent away for a woman from the Philippines, with the intention of offering marriage to her.

At the next State-wide meeting in Oklahoma City, he had searched out the fellow and asked him several pointed questions. He had been introduced to the bride, a tiny woman who barely spoke English, but who had smiled a lot and seemed happy. His buddy too, had blossomed under the woman's care. They even invited him to come and have dinner with them, when he was in the area.

So, on one of his monthly trips to Amarillo, he had made a detour and stopped in Arnett to have that visit. He was impressed with the couple, how they communicated, and how they obviously cared for one another.

A while later, he learned that another buddy of his, in Pushmataha county had been taken by a woman from Laos. She had promised to come, and when his friend had sent the money for her passage, she had just taken it and never so much as sent a thank you.

After that, he thought about it more carefully. He investigated a bit more thoroughly, and he came to the conclusion that a foreign wife might not be such a bad idea. The idea of a Russian wife became more inviting, more tantalizing. He had seen adds in a magazine by Russian women too.

Why, Russian? His Grandmother Collins was of Russian descent. She and Grandpa had raised him, and in his mind, everything good and nurturing and warm was Russian. He spoke a little of the language, too. He realized it probably was not good Russian but garnished with lots of English words and phrases. He could not write a word of it, either but Russian represented comfort and hominess. Grandma had been all of that. He realized that he missed her. She too had passed on shortly after Mary died. Grandpa had been gone several years by then.

He had lived in the house Grandpa had built, where he had been raised, until just a couple of years ago. The little house had been so comfortable and so full of all his good memories, and a few not so good, but still memorable.

One of his earliest memories was of the day the Army chaplain came to the house. He had told the family that the son, husband and father had died in a mine field in far off Korea. His mother had run from the house, screaming. His granddad had sobbed quietly, and Grandmother had been grief stricken. He had not been able to comprehend what he was being told. Surely, his strong and handsome father did not lie slaughtered in a field, like a steer at the meat processors.

One day, he did not know how long after that horrible day, he had found his mother packing her bags.

"Don't worry, Cliffy," she had said. "I'm going to be gone for a few days. I'm going to look for a job in Oklahoma City or Tulsa town or maybe Kansas City or St. Louis." She had put her bags in her car and climbed in, her pink straw hat bouncing jauntily on her curls. That was the last he had seen of her or heard from her. Well, I guess, even then this place was too far from excitement to keep a woman happy.

Cliff finally did fall asleep deeply, with rest robbing nightmares. His illusion centered around a laughing banshee, dancing about, trampling money as if it were pebbles alongside a beach. In the water were children stretching out their hands to be pulled ashore. The banshee never looked at them. He woke up, sweating, disoriented and exhausted in the gray light of early dawn.

It was time to get up, take a bracing shower, and begin the day. The coffee had stopped perking when he padded into the kitchen. Snowball and Princess were banging their bowls about in an attempt to inform him that the larder was empty. He got the message. He popped a bagel in the toaster and poured the coffee.

He wondered what time it was in Moscow? Had Katja arrived there yet? He checked the schedule. Yes, she should be at the hotel. He searched for the number, sat there holding the phone, and then, what the heck, either she is there or not. Either she is coming or not, might as well find out. He dialed. There was clicking and clicking and more clicking in the line, then ringing; one, two, three, four, five, six times. On the seventh ring, someone finally picked up. He asked if someone spoke English,

"Da!" He asked if he was connected to the Intourist Hotel.

"Da."

He asked to speak to Ekaterina Nikolayeva Novorotskaya. There was rustling as papers were being shuffled and an unbelievably harsh female voice told him she was not there. Cliff panicked. He had to talk to the woman, had to find out.

He blurted out, "Is there a reservation for Ekaterina? It's not canceled, is it?"

"Da."

"Da what? You have a reservation?"

"Da." Someone else came on the line.

"Can I help you?"

"Yes, please, I'm looking for Ekatarina Nikolayeva Novorotskaya. She has a reservation there."

"Yes, where is she coming from?"

"Sverdlovsk, I mean Yekaterinburg."

"Is she flying in?"

"No, she is taking the Trans-Siberian Train."

"Oh, she is still coming then. There is much snow, all train delayed. Maybe she come tomorrow, maybe next day. You call back." The line had gone dead.

The day passed eternally slowly for Cliff Collins. He started packing his overnight case and then decided he'd better take a couple of his good jeans and shirts to be laundered and starched.

Might as well have breakfast in town, too. That would kill some time. While in town, he figured, he might as well get some nighties and jammies for the kids and Katja.

It occurred to him on his way home after a burger at the Dairy Queen, that it might be a good idea too, to put some rolled bales of hay out into the pastures, in case it got cold. After all, he was going to be gone the best part of a week, and weather up here in the Oklahoma Panhandle can turn kind of quickly. That way, Jorge Garza, his hired help, would not have to be messing with that tractor rig he hated.

Once Cliff was finished with that chore, it was getting onto late afternoon. He needed to think about supper and to tell both Jorge and his wife Inez what to do while he was gone, so he ambled on over to the old house. He made sure that they both had his cell phone number and assured them that he would keep the phone on all the time. He asked Inez to fix the house up real nice, and if she thought something needed doing, then just do it.

"How can I make the place any nicer?" Inez had asked. "It is just about the nicest place in the county. "

"Inez, just fix it like you would want it fixed."

"Okay, Mr. Cliff. I do my best. Come stay for supper. I made cheese enchiladas. You like it how I fix them."

"Thank you, Inez. I should head up to the house. Got some packing still left to do and I want to catch the news."

"Stay, Boss. You can sleep in tomorrow. I'll do morning chores." Jorge urged him.

Cliff loved the old place they lived in. Although he was their employer, he considered them his friends too, being that insisting on proper titles for relationships was not the way to get things done in this out of the way corner of Oklahoma.

He had known these two for a long time, and so it was natural that he considered them far more than employees. His friends did not have to press him hard. The thought of staying a little longer in his former home and the idea of enchiladas made Cliff stay quite happily. Jorge and Inez lived there now, since he built the big house up on the hill, but it was the place where he had been raised, the place where he and Mary had been so happy. The place where the dream had died. The place his grandpa had built. The place he could not see go to ruin, and so he had asked those two to move in.

"I guess, I'll take you up on the offer. Inez, you're gon'na have to teach Katja how to make enchiladas. Yours are the best." He grinned like a little boy, and Jorge puffed out his chest like the compliment was his.

"My Inez, she cook good. Yes, Boss?"

The youngest daughter, Amanda, was already bringing a plate and silverware, and the oldest granddaughter was bringing a chair, and everyone at the table just scooted a little tighter together.

Once home, Cliff Collins had seen to his pets, and while shining his good boots, he had watched CNN. The Weather Channel had talked of heavy snowfall east of the Volga River. There was talk of the transportation network being bogged down by all the snow. The good news was that the weekly Trans-Siberian Train was running about thirty-six hours behind schedule and should arrive in Moscow any moment now. Cliff had gotten out the atlas and followed the weather map intently.

He hoped that the train in which Katja was traveling, had cleared that obstacle. Otherwise, she would miss her plane, and he'd be stuck in Dallas for God knows how long. He did not like cities. They closed in on him, and he felt claustrophobic, overwhelmed by all the people. It was okay to visit in the big towns for a day or two, but much longer, and he grew nervous, so, he finished packing. Then he sat thinking for a long while.

Chapter Three

Why had he ever build this junior mansion? He loved the little house down by the road so much, the house where Inez and Jorge now lived, but this house was good, too, and since neither he nor Katja would have emotional baggage attached to this house, perhaps they could make it their own. He hoped so.

Building the new house up on the mesa overlooking a small gorge through which the Cimarron flowed had been the culmination of many forces. His accountant and his friends' urgings had something to do with it. So had the realization that most women would not want to move into the little house. The ceilings were low, the rooms small and boxy, and the kitchen had been upgraded the last time in 1958. There was no rhyme or reason to the warren of rooms, just that they were needed and so had been added on, as the need arose. Bathrooms were small and old, and closet space had been at a premium, even when he was a youngster.

Noah Wyllie, his accountant, had advised him to take on some debt. "A new house would be the best. You need that tax deduction. Otherwise, in another year, your dividend earnings are taking you into such a high bracket, that you lose most of them to the IRS. Think about putting some of your money into tax exempt bonds, and get yourself an IRA or Keogh or some sort of tax shelter. A new big mortgage would sure be helpful."

"I don't like owing anybody any money. If I build me a new house, I'll pay for in cash. I won't have some loan shark hanging over my head every time the price of a barrel of oil goes down a penny. You know that, Noah. Start thinking about investments, and make me a plan. I got to be going now. Come by, when you have something to talk to me about."

"Paying for a new house might not be such a bad idea, either. That would reduce that big fat bank account a bit, and you would not have the interest earnings from that, either. Yeah, that might do the trick, unorthodox, but feasible." So the idea of the new house was born.

Cliff knew where he wanted to build the new house, on his most favorite spot on the whole ranch. The good thing was that the spot was just a few hundred yards from the barn and tool shed. So he called out Hollis Webber, the builder and remodeler, over from Guymon. That guy had done a lot of work in Beaver county, too. He had also done some work in Cimarron county.

He chuckled. Yeah, he remembered the day when Hollis crawled out of his beat up pick-up truck and had sat next to him in the other recliner in the old living room.

"Cliff, now tell me, what kind of house have you got in mind?"

"A new one."

"I figured as much. How big do you need it to be?"

Cliff studied that question for a while and found no answer. "I guess about the size this one is."

"How many bedrooms do you need?" Another question Cliff could not answer or the number of bathrooms required. The questioning went on and on. In the end, the plan for the house was tabled until Cliff had an idea of what he wanted.

He had talked to his friends and to Jorge and Inez and to Don and, of course, Donna, who advised him to talk to a few women.

"You want to have a bride one day again. Better fix it from a woman's point of view." That made sense, some, but he was going to live there too.

Donna came up with a splendid idea. "Visit with some of the realtors down in Amarillo and in the city when you go there, and see what is in style now. Buy yourself a few home magazines to give you ideas." And so, he did.

The new house consumed his mind. Don and Donna's son came up from Houston and brought a bunch of house plans with him. He explained what they were building in The Woodlands and down around Katy. Donnie showed him plans of the Hill country prize winning architecture.

Donnie was talking of lots of options, a wine cellar, a master suite, a study, and a safe room, or a storm cellar in the garage. Did he need a den big enough for a pool table? Certainly, he'd want a smart house where he could turn the heat on from his cell phone, when he was coming in from a long day out in the field. Or where he could monitor Inez from his laptop when he was away in the city. He might also want motion detectors all around the house to let him know when someone was around, and of course, he needed several bedrooms for his guests. The thing to do there was to have a Jack and Jill bathroom arrangement. He'd also want a Jacuzzi tub in his bath and maybe a sauna.

Cliff's head was swimming, but talking with young Donnie had the effect to shape his mind and give him some concrete ideas. On his next shopping trip to town, he made that appointment with the realtor and traipsed for a long afternoon through every available house in Amarillo. The new house was taking shape in his mind.

After a long year of planning and building, he finally moved in. In just a short time, he began to realize the amenities he'd resisted so where actually enjoyable, and in quite a few instances, a blessing. With Donna's help, he furnished the place spartanly. He wanted his bride to really decorate their home. He did bring some of the pieces from the old place along, those that could be called antiques and that had some value and some style.

For three years now, the new house had been his abode, his home. If things went all right, he should be sharing his home with his new family in about a week.

Finding the woman to share the home with Cliff had been an adventure in futility. Eventually, persistence had paid off, and Lady Fortune had come to his aid. On his annual visit to the doctor about four years ago, he had first seen a magazine that published pictures of women who wanted to come to the United States with the object of marrying the person who'd send for them. Like choosing a nice shirt out of the

Sears and Roebuck catalog, he had scoffed, and then, he had surreptitiously taken the old copy with him and studied all the photographs there. A surprising number of women were very pretty. Others were very young. He felt for these girls, hoping that their disillusion with life would not come true. Other women had children or were older, widows without a chance for new happiness in their circumstances.

Cliff was saddened and fascinated by the pictures. He scrutinized each picture and story carefully but found none that were appealing to him. For days, he scoured the stories, just to learn or see what could be deciphered and what was written between the lines.

On a visit to Liberal, Kansas, he stopped by a magazine seller and looked for a newer copy but could not bring himself to purchase one. He was not quite that desperate, he told himself. He kept searching for magazines in unexpected spots.

Eventually, he broke down and bought one. Six months later, he bought another. He really did not know what he was looking for, but he kept it up. Time passed. He felt more comfortable in his new home, but he hadn't had a date in years.

On a trip to the city last April, he found a four-month-old copy in the men's room and took that magazine home with him. Once home, the magazine languished unread in his pick-up.

While waiting for the county agent to come along, Cliff had picked the paper up and thumped through the well-worn and now dirty pages. One of the pictures in the bottom third of a page had him suddenly mesmerized. He put the magazine down, closed it, and shuffled the pages again. The same page fell open again.

The woman was smiling shyly. She had her arms around two children, a little boy and girl, the girl still a toddler. The woman looked to be in her thirties, old, to have such young children. There was something endearing about her. Cliff did not know what was so fascinating, but the picture called to him. When Bob Hancock, the county agent, drove up, Cliff was barely able to pay attention to him.

A week, later that picture was still on his mind. He was fantasizing about the woman and dreaming about her. He went to the photo shop to see if they could blow up the picture a bit. They did, but it now became fuzzy.

Cliff Collins became obsessed with the woman and her children. The little boy looked so serious, so mature. Yet he could not be more than five years old. The little girl looked like a china doll. She had blond, curly hair to her brother's straight, dark tresses. Reading the little story that came with the picture only helped to make up Cliff's mind. The woman did not want so much, just the chance for her children to have an education. She would like to have a better way of life, a private bathroom for the family and her own kitchen and a bedroom for the children to share. That was all she was hoping for. Well, he could provide that and more.

So, after long ruminations on the subject, and a couple of conversations with Snowball and Princess, brought him to the astute conclusion that he should mail a letter to this woman Ekatarina Nikolayeva Novorotskaya.

Although Cliff Collins had no trouble expressing himself, there were numerous false starts, and the trash can besides his desk was full to overflowing when he finally finished the letter. In it, he talked candidly about himself, his circumstances, and that he was considered financially stable and comfortable. He offered to bring Ekaterina to the States with her children.

In his letter to her, he wrote, *"If it is agreeable with you, I should like to have you here before Christmas. So, the children can enjoy the season. Please answer as soon as possible, so I might make the pertinent arrangements. Should you not be interested, please be so kind and let me know. I will send recompense for your troubles."*

Then, the waiting started. All of September passed without any word from Russia. October came, and with it, the first cold winds from the Rockies. Cliff was depressed. He wanted to hear from Russia.

He wanted a positive answer. His whole being longed to share his days with the sad looking, pretty woman in that picture.

One day in mid-October, he received a call that changed his life.

"This is Minnie down at the post office. There is a letter here for you, Cliff, with some really weird stamps. I can't even make out where it's from, and the return address is in some screwy writing. If you want that letter today, you best get down here. Roger, our mail carrier, is not going to get past your place till late, if at all."

Cliff had jumped into his truck and raced to Boise City in record time, but he could not rip open the letter in front of Minnie's prying eyes, and so he flew home again. The tires barely touched the ground, and with his two animals in attendance, he ripped the letter open. After just a few words, he started to whoop and holler and dance about the room, laughing and crying all at once. "Yes, they are coming!"

Chapter Four

That is how it all started. Now, Clifford Collins was standing in the International Arrivals Terminal at Dallas/Fort Worth International Airport clutching a bunch of roses and hoping to see the people for whom he was waiting. He'd been there for over an hour now.

The plane had landed almost forty-five minutes ago, but passengers only trickled out of the small door opposite his waiting spot. There was a barrier dividing the room. He did not know why. The waiting room was almost empty now. He had a good view of the door the arrivals had come through. He knew immigration would interview and possibly search the passengers, but what was taking them so long?

He was just about the last person waiting, when the door opened and a very tiny girl with blond, curly hair came out. She wore a heavy red parka, and over that a backpack about to crush her. She pulled along the suitcase on wheels, which Cliff recognized. He smiled big, and as he did, little Irina dropped her bag and came running towards him.

"It's me, Papi! Rina! We're here." Cliff spread his arms, and she rushed into them. He lifted her up, kissed her cheek, and was indescribably happy. Seconds later, her brother emerged from the room beyond the door.

"Rina, you dummy, you don't know ..." His voice faltered as he saw the happy faces of both. Aleksandr picked up Rina's suitcase on his way to meet Cliff Collins.

Cliff saw the serious face of the little boy and his appraising manner. The kid was scared and worried, he realized.

"Hi, Aleksandr, welcome to America. I am so glad you came." He smiled big at the child and tussled his hair just a little. Some of the apprehension seemed to leave the child.

Finally Katja appeared, looking tired, worn out, loaded down with a back pack and two rolling bags and the heavy down coat he had sent. All he wanted to do was help her and hold her. She was so tiny, and frail looking, under all she was carrying. And beautiful, he realized. *She is tiny, dark-haired, even fragile-looking*, he thought. He had expected a solid looking woman of Slavic heritage. This woman looked nothing like the stout women he had seen in news pictures.

This woman looked like a ballerina, tiny and trim and beautiful. She even had her hair pulled back in a bun like a dancer, but some of her curls had come loose during the long voyage and now framed her face with softening ringlets. She had dark eyes, but from that distance, he could not tell what they were. A second later, as she came forward, he realized the eyes were a very dark blue. *Absolutely extraordinary*, was his assessment. She was so beautiful; it took his breath away and made him feel clumsy and awkward.

Katja had spotted Cliff at the same time. Her first thought was *Oh my God, he is so big. How am I to handle that? Is he that big all over? But he really is handsome looking.* That was her next thought, and he had the children. He rushed forward to help her and to press his flowers into her hand.

"Welcome, Ekaterina, to America. Thank you for coming, Katja. You make me very happy." He put his arm about her, hugged her to him, and just kissed her hair a little. In that moment, all her concerns vanished.

"Thank you, Mr. Collins. I am glad we came,

too." Her English was heavily accented, not like the children's. Where had they learned English so well?

"Are you hungry or thirsty, or do you need to find a bathroom? Is everybody well?"

"Da, ah, yes."

"We go home now, Papi?"

"No, not today, little one. Today, we rest, and tomorrow, we will go shopping, and in a few days, we go home, okay?"

"Da."

"Sasha, you're hungry?"

"Nyet, thirsty, Mr. Collins."

"What would you like to drink ice tea, Coke, milk, juice, Seven Up?"

A shy little smile washed across his face, hopeful, wistful, expectant. "May I have some Coca Cola, please, Mr. Collins?"

"Sure, just a minute. There is a little snack bar just up ahead. And you, Irina, would you like something too?" He had turned to the little girl.

"Orange juice, is better for us, yes, Mama?"

Katja smiled, "You may have whatever Mr. Collins offers."

"Orange juice, it is then, and for you Katja, maybe something a little stronger?"

"Oh no, tea would be wonderful."

"Iced tea or hot tea?" Katja was bewildered. Iced tea, what was that?

"Hot tea is maybe better, is cold outside."

"Oh no, it is quite warm outside. The temperature is around eighty degrees." Katja looked at him, uncomprehending.

"Mama I am so hot; may I take my coat off?" The little girl was wriggling in Cliff's arms.

"Nyet, Rina, we will be going outside soon and it is winter out there, although I have never seen the sun look so warm in December."

"Mama, I am hot too. Please let us take our coats off."

Cliff had to interrupt. "Katja, I think the children are right. It is quite warm in here, and outside it is even warmer. You might want to take your coat off, too. The temperature is around eighty degrees Fahrenheit outside. That is, let me think, about eighteen to twenty degrees Celsius. Maybe a little less. Certainly, warm enough to go without a coat."

The look of surprise on Katja's face was precious. "But is winter. We had several meters of snow in our village, and there was snow in Moskva too."

"Yes, it is winter, but Dallas is further south than the Crimea. It hardly ever snows here, and then only a little bit, and it melts right away. Let the children take off the warm clothing. And you too." Reluctantly Katja permitted the request. She, too, removed the warm coat she was wearing. He told the children to stuff mittens, muffler, and hat into the pockets and then he strapped the garments to their suitcases.

He got everyone their drinks, including a big iced tea for himself. Cliff showed Katja how to doctor her drink to her preference. A porter was hailed and all the luggage stored on a trolley. Slowly they made their way to the big glass doors.

Passengers and their vehicles were clogging the road outside the terminal. People were streaming across the street in search of their own vehicles in the parking garages. Others were taking the parking lot train to long term parking. It was pleasantly cool in the building. When the big automatic doors opened to let a traveler into the building, Katja was hit by a blast of hot air. It surprised her, although she had been expecting a comfortable temperature.

"It's hotter outside than in here. What makes it so?"

Cliff was surprised himself. She did not know about air conditioning. He tried to explain about that, His Russian however did not include that kind of technical knowledge, and Katja's English was not complete enough for her to understand. Then, they were on the pavement, and Sasha was fascinated with the number of vehicles around him.

"Mama, there are more cars here than in all of Russia. Look at them all! Where are the people who own them? Are they there for everyone's use?"

"I don't know, Aleksandr. Surely not."

"Papi, do you have a car like these?" Irina was just as curious as her brother.

"Yes, it's parked a little further over there."

"Is it like this one?" She pointed to a bright red, little Ford Focus.

"No, it's a little bigger, and it's green."

Her eyes got huge in surprise and disbelief. "Bigger?"

"Yes, right over there, see?" Cliff walked between a big green Navigator parked next to a small green Grand Am. He hit the door button on his key chain and opened the rear passenger door. Handing the little girl into the vehicle, he asked her to sit in the far booster seat. When he turned around to help Katja into the vehicle, he found, to his surprise, that Katja and Sasha were not right behind him. Bewilderment confused him momentarily, and then Cliff realized that they were standing by the passenger doors of the green Pontiac.

"Over here, you two. This is our truck." He helped the boy into his seat and showed him how to buckle up, and then he opened the front passenger door and helped Katja in and showed her how to use the seatbelt. The porter had by this time stowed all the luggage in the rear compartment. Cliff paid him. Finally, he strapped Irina into her booster seat, showed everyone where their drink holders were and then climbed in himself.

Soon, they were out of the parking garage and on their way to the airport exit and highway 183. Rush hour in the Dallas-Fort Worth Metroplex had started. Highway 183, being a major artery connecting the two cities and several suburbs, was at its usual snail's pace.

The children and Katja were agog at the amount of traffic on the road. Cliff himself did not feel that comfortable with the congestion on the roadway. He lived, after all, outside of Boise City, Oklahoma, where ten cars on Highway 287 in front of the court house constitute a major traffic jam. It was good that he had made the trip to the Airport and back to the hotel last night once, when traffic was lighter. Now, he at least he knew which lane of traffic he had to be, to find his way back to their hotel.

As they mounted the high access lanes to Highway 360, he pointed out the downtown areas of both cities, Dallas to the left and south, and Ft. Worth to the right. Katja wanted to see homes, asked how many families lived in the apartment complexes besides the road, and how large those families normally are. Cliff had no idea but supposed that each balcony area indicated one apartment, and that one unit would be inhabited by no more than one family or a married couple or maybe two roommates.

"Would you like to see what an apartment looks like? We can stop by tomorrow and check one out."

Katja was enthusiastic about that. Living conditions were of great concern to her. Although the going was slow, it did not take very long to arrive at their lodging. He had booked rooms on the top floor for the view and quiet. Having the elevator to ride was novel for the children. Carpeted halls were something too fantastic to imagine. The children pushed into the room.

Aleksandr instantly saw the TV. Little Irina was surprised by the bathroom dressing area. Cliff had kept the door open to the adjoining room, and the children were now cautiously exploring the other room. Another bathroom, two huge beds, and a little table with easy chairs and wonder of wonders, another television was in that room.

"All this for just us?" Irina was dumbfounded, and Sasha was looking for a way to turn on the tube. Cliff helped him, explained the remote and left the child to his own devices. Soon the boy was happily clicking through the channels. Irina found the stuffed Panda bear and the clothes Cliff had laid out on one of the beds. Her shriek of surprise brought everyone running.

"Thank you, Papi, thank you." She tackled Cliff in a bear hug somewhere above the knees. Katja too thanked Cliff and then busied herself with her flowers and the vase she had found waiting on the bedside stand. Cliff in the meantime brought up the last bit of luggage. There was another joyous cry from the children's room.

"Mama, look, it's *Texas Ranger!* They have it here too." The boy was quite happy for something familiar, although here, it was in English. Sasha had not mastered that much of the language yet, so he was concentrating quite intensely. When Cliff brought in the children's luggage, he saw the little boy's fascination.

105

"Do you like that show?"

"Yes, Mr. Collins, I watch all the time with Sergey at home."

"Would you like to see where they filmed it?" Sasha looked puzzled.

"Would you like to see the courthouse where the rangers worked, where their office was?"

"Is real?" Sasha was puzzled. "You can go see? Is not Hollywood?"

"No, it's not Hollywood. It's a real courthouse, only Walker, Trevette and Ms. Cahill never worked there as rangers. We can see it today. Would you like that?"

"Oh, yes," he breathed.

"Okay then. We go to Ft. Worth and have supper at Sundance Square after we take a look at the courthouse."

The boy was running with excitement through the two rooms, whooping and hollering like a banshee. He was thinking that Mr. Collins might just be fine after all. He certainly would write to Oleg and Sergey.

"Katja, would you like to rest a little, or are

you hungry? What would you like to do? If we go to Ft. Worth, it will take a little while before we have something to eat. I can pick up some snacks for the meantime."

"I think I'd like to freshen up a bit. It was so hot in that room at the Airport, and here too. Then we can go."

"Oh, forgive me. I forgot to turn the air on." With that, he turned the knobs on their window unit and cool, fresh air started to circulate. "Is that better?"

"Oh, yes, thank you, very much, yes. Mr. Collins, how did you do that? What makes it instantly cooler in this room?" Katja was baffled. They had similar window units in the hotel in Russia, but they provided only heat for the room.

Cliff was equally as mystified. She really did not know about air conditioning. He could not imagine life without it. So, he patiently explained and demonstrated, hot and cold air coming from the unit. He explained that everyone had some sort of cooling system here in the South. The northern States were not as dependent on air conditioning for comfort, but even there, many homes and most businesses had it.

Little Irina had caught the drift of the conversation. Mama was making herself pretty.

"Mama, may I wear the pretty things that Papi

gave me? My old stuff is all dirty."

Sasha, too, looked longingly at the jeans and T-shirt Mr. Collins had provided for him.

"Da, I think that might be fine, if Mr. Collins agrees. You might ask him."

Cliff just smiled and nodded his head. Katja, too was examining the clothing she found spread on that enormous bed. *A shower and fresh clean clothes would be so revitalizing,* Katja thought. Only what would she do with her stubborn, curly hair? Cliff caught her struggle. He told her he liked her curls, but if she wanted them to behave a certain way, maybe his gel would help her achieve the result she wanted.

The children enlisted Cliff to help them with their baths and getting dressed while Katja did the same. Katja was amazed how well everything fit. She combed Rina's hair and Cliff worked on the boy. With Cliff's assistance, she was able to mold her own unruly tresses into a smooth coif with a small bun in the back.

On their way back to the vehicle, Cliff Collins observed his new family with pride. They were beautiful, well behaved children, and Katja was exquisite. Tomorrow, he would see to it that she had her hair done to her liking and bought a little make up to enhance those lovely eyes and cheekbones. He wanted to hug them all, take her in his arms, hold her, kiss her. He felt a physical need for that but wondered, if he was rushing things a bit. He knew he would have to be patient. Katja came from a different world, where sex was not expected at the end of an evening. Yet, his need to hold her was so powerful. He could almost not resist it. Irina was a good substitute. Her, he could hold and even give a little peck on the cheek.

The evening turned out wonderfully. Cliff could feel the reserve draining out of the boy. Once, he had almost called him Papi. He had not expected that for a long time in the future. All evening, Katja had smiled a most radiant, happy smile at him. He felt good.

For Katja, the evening brought one surprise after another unbelievable surprise. Mr. Collins, although very big and tall by her standards, was also incredible handsome, and more importantly, thoughtful and kind. The roses he had handed her were just the first indication of his generosity. The clothes he had waiting for them, had made her think of her husband, who had never been able to even pick up a pair of socks that fit. How had this man managed to find attractive and fitting clothing for them all?

Then, there was the patience he used to explain unfamiliar things to her and the children and the attention with which he showered them. Taking Sasha to that big, pink building and then having the policeman show them the rooms that had been used for the actual filming, would go a very long way to

109

endear him to her son.

She, too, had felt the confidence building in Sasha towards Mr. Collins. How Irina was able to trust him completely and unreservedly was still unfathomable to her, but evidently, her daughter had found something in his picture that led her to trust him, and so far, he had not disappointed them in the least.

Katja, too, felt herself drawn to Cliff. His actions and his physical appearance appealed to her greatly. She was, however, not ready to have sexual relations with him. The scepter of such intimacy hung over her as something to dread. Would he expect that tonight? There was only the one big bed in their room. She could go and sleep with the children. Would she displease him with that move? Or should she just be passive and let happen what will? Yet, she knew too, that she was beginning to be physically attracted by him. When he had helped her with her hair, for a moment, she had wanted to lean back against him and have him hold her. Then, she held herself in check. That move would certainly be thought as being too forward. Would he lose respect for her if she gave him a peck on the cheek?

She liked the man enough not to want to endanger any part of their developing relationship. There was just so little she knew about him or about customs concerning relationships in America. All she had ever heard was that American women were so loose as to be considered almost as whores. He certainly would not want that from his future wife. Was that not why he had send for her?

Katja was not sure of his motives to invite her and the children to share his life. She herself had not expected the man to be as attractive nor as pleasant at all. She could not understand why he had been unable to find a wife among American women.

They were all so beautiful, and his qualities would have to be appreciated by anyone. What was she missing here? Would he turn into a monster once they got to his home? She could not fathom that. His behavior was too natural to be contrived. Perhaps, he liked his vodka too much, and like some of her friends at home, would become belligerent when he was drunk, but he did not have the look of someone who drank more than was good for him, no red nose, no flushed face. Katja was sure of that. I can hit myself over the head worrying about all of this, but only time will provide the answers. *For the time being, I should be happy with what fate has handed me. Let me just enjoy this,* she thought.

After exploring the Tarrant County Court House, Cliff had taken his new family to Sundance Square where they had dinner on the upstairs terrace of the one good French cuisine restaurant. On the way back to the hotel, the children had seen the Christmas decorations proliferating in all the front yards and not a few backyards along the shores of Lake Arlington.

Cliff had been very surprised that they knew nothing of Santa Claus.

Katja had explained that the celebration of religious holidays had been forbidden in Russia during the Communist area. Now, most people had forgotten that once there had been such celebrations. She had readily agreed, when he suggested, they all would go see some of the decorations.

When he suggested that they all celebrate the holiday at his home in Oklahoma, she was truly astonished. He would go to such extremes for her children. How absolutely marvelous! Would she mind helping him with putting up a tree and decorating it? It was a lot of work, he had admitted, and would she be able to bake some cookies for the children to leave for St. Nick? Katja promised to do all, but he would please tell her what to do and what was expected. He told her that there were no set rules, just watch and learn and get into the swing of things. He felt sure, the children would have no problem in deciding what should be done.

She had as much fun as the children seeing, all the decorations and the expense to which people had gone, just so others could admire their fantasies. Katja had noted that Cliff, too, had a good time. The children had been absolutely in awe of all they had seen.

She had thought the little ones would soon fall

asleep, but they astounded her with their enthusiasm. Irina was fascinated with the homes they saw. She kept wanting to know what her Papi's house looked like. Cliff tried to tell her, show her examples. Katja finally told her that these houses where most likely occupied by more than one family, just like the dacha at home. Had they not seen several Christmas trees in some of the houses. Cliff, however, had insisted repeatedly, that only one family lived in these mansions and that his home was of similar style and size. This Katja found totally unbelievable, so she remained somewhat skeptical. Eventually, they had seen all they could. The children were tired.

On their way back to the hotel, Katja remembered that she needed to wash clothing. All of her and the children's things were soiled. She hated to break the festive mood prevailing in the vehicle, but she must.

"Is there any place where I can wash some things for the children and myself. All our clothing has been worn and needs to be cleaned. If it's permissible, I can wash some things in the sink in the hotel and hang them to dry in the bathrooms."

"Oh, my gosh, I should have thought of that. I told you not to bring so many clothes. Well, I guess you could wash some undies in the sink at the hotel, but that's just not necessary. Let's go and get what you all need. I just hate to wake the little ones to go into a store."

"No, Papi, we don't have any other clothes. We brought all we got. Mami even had to go and buy some clothes for Sasha and me, so we'd have clean clothes to get here. We could have put some more into our backpacks, but we did not have anymore."

Katja would have liked for her to shut up. There was no use in that. Cliff would find out how few clothes they had. Nonetheless, she felt embarrassed.

Cliff sensed her embarrassment. "There's a Target over there. Let's just stop by. They have everything you'll need." He pulled into a parking space.

To Katja, the store seemed enormous. Even the famous GUM in Moscow could not be as large as this store. Cliff put the children into a huge red basket with wheels and then showed her through the store. He let her browse in the lady's department and watched to see at which items she really looked and then put back again.

Once she was finished in the Ladies section, he took her over to the little girl's section. He had whispered to little Irina to keep her mother busy. It took only a few moments for him to pick up the items Katja had returned and to secret them in the cart. Rina had done a wonderful job, and now she begged her Papi for some of those cute things she was seeing. Of course, Cliff could not deny her anything. It really was not so much. A package of undies and a couple of really frilly ones. The same for socks and of course two more nighties and some T-shirts, both long and short sleeved. A pair of jeans with embroidery and a matching top. The little girl was hugging things to her. The smile she gave Cliff was worth every last penny he spent.

Then, they all went to the Boy's department. Sasha was trying to be frugal. He had an idea of how much money they had spent so far. At least, he knew, that at home, Mama would have never been able to buy all these many clothes at once. He tried to demure. Cliff however told the youngster that he was sure Sasha too, needed quite a few things.

"Besides," Cliff told him, "I really don't want to ask your little sister for help in what you need and like."

Finally, the child had what he needed, underwear and socks, jeans and tops enough for four days and some more sleepers.

"Now, let's go and find some sneakers for you guys."

"What is sneakers, Papi?"

"Shoes, a kind of shoe that is very comfortable."

"Mr. Collins, you have bought so much already. The cart is full. Here, I have some of your dollars left. You spoil them too much."

"Nonsense. Now let's go back and find you some clothes, not just underwear. You will need them." She looked exasperated. The cost of all these purchases were mounting to levels which Katja could not comprehend.

"Oh, let me, Katja. I'm having so much fun! You keep your money, and when you run out, let me know. I never want you to be without a few dollars in your pocket." He put in quite seriously.

The children did fall asleep on the way home. Katja, too, was sleepy.

"I should have just washed some things. You spend so very much." She groused.

"No, Sweets, this was not so much. It gave me pleasure. You have had a few very exhausting weeks. You need to rest and have a little fun. Tomorrow, we will do some more shopping, and I want you to go and have your hair done. You are so beautiful, and you deserve a little pampering and luxury. I am just happy I can do a little for you." He reached over and gently squeezed her hand and smiled at her.

She looked over to him and smiled. There

where teardrops forming in the corners of her eyes. She did not know what to say, how to express her feeling.

"Thank you, Mr. Collins. You do so much for us already. I not want us to be a…" she searched for a word, then settled on "trouble."

"You're no trouble and no burden. I love doing these little things. I hope you will forgive me, but I'm having so much fun. And..." he let the word trail "would you call me Cliff, please?"

"If you like, Mr. Col....er... I mean, Cliff. I always think of you as Mr. Collins. Is going to take a little while to get comfortable, Mr. C..., Cliff."

Upon their return to the hotel, Katja put the sleeping children to bed. Both had woken long enough to help her in undressing them. While she was doing that, Cliff had taken the opportunity to change into his pajamas also. That was a novel and uncomfortable thing for him. At home, he mostly just put on the bottoms and a T-shirt. He was pouring champagne into glasses when Katja stepped out of the bathroom, clad in her new silky gown and matching housecoat.

"A toast to us, Katja". He said as he handed her a flute.

"Yes, to us."

"We're going to be all right, Sweetheart." He said with more confidence than he felt at that moment. Katja only nodded. He put his arm around her.

"I only hope you don't find me too ugly to like."

Katja was so tired. The champagne only made her more tired. She had heard his fear in his voice and could honestly answer.

"No, no, not ugly, very handsome. Yes, you're very handsome and good to me. Only so big. Is a little frightening, da?"

"You really think I'm frightening?"

"No, just so big. I'm thinking, I too little." She was so tired, she could not think anymore. She'd been awake for more than thirty hours. The words just tumbled out without much thought and heavily accented.

"Nobody ever found me too big. Mary never complained, and she was just about as tiny as you are."

"I sorry, who Mary?"

"My wife."

Katja's face fell, shock registered everywhere.

"You married, have wife?"

"No, no, Mary died twenty years ago, but she was very small, like you."

"Oooh, good." she smiled, then apologized, "Not mean it like that. Good you not married now. I not want to share you with wife." She laughed hysterically
.

A grin spread across his face too. "You really like me a little?"

"Da, much."

This time he hugged her a bit tighter. "We're gonne be okay, Katja. I like you much, too."

"Good."

"Come, sit down, maybe in bed. You must be tired. When did you get up today?"

"Da, very tired, no sleep maybe thirty-two hours, I think, maybe more."

He pulled the covers down for her and fluffed up pillows, stacking them so she could sit comfortably.

"I tried to get a suite with two beds in each room. They did not have that. Only suites with two beds in one room. I'm sorry. It's a bit awkward, but I wanted you to be able to walk into the children's room from our room and not have to go out into the hall. I know, that would be far too scary for them, to be totally separated from you might upset them. I thought, I could sleep here on the recliner, or on the sofa."

"No, is not need. Bed is so big, is room for you, too." She smiled at him and tried to move over.

"Thanks, Sweets, later, maybe. Tell me, was the train trip hard? How come you did not get to Moscow on time? It really worried me." He could not let her sleep just yet. He needed to talk to her. He needed to know that she was happy with him. He had seen that quick expression on her face when she first entered the waiting room. Was it fear? Or was it repulsion? He hoped not.

"Oh my," Katja's hands flew to her face. "I sorry, I forgot. I am to tell you greetings from your friends."

"My friends? I know no one in Russia." Now, it was his turn to be bewildered.

"Yes, yes, Mr. and Mrs. Martin, your friends. Tell me all about you. Mrs. Martin, say you sleep in big hat." She giggled.

"Martin, in Russia? No, I'm sure I don't

know."

"Da, Nigel and Deena Martin and children. You know, from England." He was totally confused now.

"I didn't see them get off the plane, why did they not say hello? They're back in the States? How nice! We have to get together with them."

"No, no, no, Mi... Cliff. Not on plane, on train to Moskva. They at next table in dining room. Children meet, then we too. They in next compartment on train too. Children play, Deena talk to me. She have Russian. She asked where I going. I tell, we talk more. She think, you friend. Call husband. Yes, is friend. We talk more. Heather, she play teacher, teach Sasha and Rina much English."

"You mean Nigel Martin, the petroleum engineer, is in Russia now? What is he doing there? But what a coincidence that you met in Russia! What is he doing there?"

"He work for British Petroleum some place deep in Siberia. Not tell where. Maybe better not say. They were on their way home to England but wanted to spend a few days in Moskva and St. Petersburg. They very nice people and children so good and smart."

Katja just fell asleep sitting up in bed. Her

head dropped to one side, her eyes closed, and she mumbled;

"Must sleep now. Good night, Mr. Cliff."

Cliff felt for her. He pulled one of the pillows from behind her, let her rest on the other and covered her. Then he made himself comfortable on the recliner. He hoped he could sleep.

He must have fallen into slumber for he woke as someone placed a blanket over him. He was disoriented. Finally, he realized that it was Katja, who was making sure that he was warm.

"Oh, good, you wake. Come to bed, Mr. Collins. Is not good sleeping like that. Bed plenty big."

"Katja, no, I can't. I might take advantage of you. I want to wait till we both are ready. It's too soon."

"Mr. Clifford Collins, you good man", she kissed him on the mouth, quickly. "Is okay, you must sleep, no matter, come sleep. She took the blanket off again and spread it on the bed. Then she took his hand and led him to bed. She crawled in on the other side and turned her back to him and was instantly asleep again.

Cliff lay there for a bit, stiff, uncomfortable, but when her breathing turned deep and regular, he too, turned to his side, with his back towards her and fell into deep refreshing slumber. He also had a few very stressful days.

Cliff woke late the next morning. He found himself hugging Katja to himself. She still had her back towards him, but she was holding on to his arms with unexpected strength. She had her leg over his. Carefully, he extricated himself. God only knew what he would do, if he stayed like that for any length of time. Surely, the children would be waking soon. He got up, took a cold shower and dressed. When he came back into the room, Katja was awake. He wished her a pleasant day and inquired whether she liked coffee or tea in the morning,

"I'm going to get us some at the front office and some juice for the children."

"Mr. Cliff, you show me how to make water hot for bath, please?"

"Sure."

When he came back with the drinks, Katja had showered and dressed. She was fussing with her hair, asked if she could use more of his wonderful gel. The children too were waking up.

By 8:30 A.M., they were seated in a booth at

the IHOP next door. The breakfast choices were mind boggling to Cliff's new family. He finally suggested they all order something different, and everyone share. Rina was only sure that she wanted real strawberries. Sasha too, was tempted by the fruit, but he also thought that he wanted to taste bacon and sausages. Cliff ordered side orders of the meats and scrambled eggs, biscuits and gravy for himself, an omelet for Katja and waffles for the children. Everyone loved their food. Sausages and bacon disappeared. Everyone was happily chatting between bites.

On their way to the Galleria, they stopped by some apartments. He explained his request to the lady at the rental office, and she was helpful enough to show them two furnished models. Katja and the children were impressed, although, to Cliff it felt like he was stepping into modified shoe boxes.

Traffic was a little lighter at mid-morning than what they experienced yesterday afternoon, and it took no time at all to reach Loop 12 and the connection to Stemmons Freeway. LBJ freeway was still busy. Surprisingly, the traffic only slowed; there were no stoppages. They arrived at the shopping center just after ten in the morning. They even lucked into a covered parking space.

Cliff's new family was enthralled when they saw the ice rink. A coach was coaxing his charges through, what used to be called, school figures, telling them that without the basics, those dreamed of quads would never happen.

Katja was dropped off at the beauty shop at Macy's, and then Cliff took the children to the toy stores to show them the undreamed-of wonders to be found within. He purchased coloring books and activity books, Crayolas, puzzles, and beginner books, everything he could think of to teach the children their numbers and alphabet and English words. He found a couple of CDs with children's songs to sing along and three books on tape of fairy tales. Then, it was time to pick up their mother.

Katja looked stunning. At the makeup counters, he had her pick what she would like, and with the help of one of the professionals there, she was turned into a beauty to make even the most successful model jealous.

Chapter Five

The next two days flew by in a whirl of shopping, going to the zoo, the aquarium, and the experience of Christmas in the Park at Six Flags. Friday evening, Cliff made arrangements with one of the desk clerks at the hotel to baby sit the children while he took Katja out to an intimate dinner at a jazz club and dancing.

Saturday was devoted to groceries. In the morning, they shopped for staples and anything Katja was accustomed to having in Russia. There was precious little. At Central Market in Plano, they found sausages and rye bread. At a bookstore, they found English - Russian dictionaries. They were both delighted and had the library-sized one shipped to the ranch.

At *Sur-la-Table*, Katja purchased a waffle iron, electric. How wonderful is that, to have waffles almost instantly! That along with some electronic scales was also shipped. So was a blender and a juicer as well as a bread machine. Several calls to the ranch ascertained the fact that only an old hand mixer existed. A new one was obtained and a small chopper for onions, peppers and the like. Finally, Inez insisted, that if Katja was to make cookies, she needed a good food processor.

Katja was objecting to every work-saving appliance, for she could see the dollars adding up. She was appalled by the money Cliff was spending. She was afraid he was bankrupting himself in his desire to have everything that one could ever think of having, as far as kitchen appliances were concerned. The huge order was shipped to the ranch. Even Katja realized they could not cram all the purchases into their vehicle.

After supper that Saturday, Cliff took them all shopping for more perishable items. The children had discovered pizza the previous evening. Sasha found the boxes of enticing goodies in the frozen food isle. Both children were begging for the goodies. Besides that, they purchased bacon, sausages, butter, apples, oranges, bananas and some cabbages.

Later that evening Katja helped with packing the vehicle for departure. All of their dirty clothes were crammed into the backpacks, to be secured to the roof top carrier, along with a couple of the suit cases. Sacks of clothing were combined to be stuffed into nooks and crannies. Shoes, books and smaller toys wound up under the seats. The big heavy coats, they had worn upon arrival, where folded neatly beneath the booster seats for optimal space and extra height for the children.

Cliff had two ice chests, which could be plugged into the cigarette lighters, and these were stored behind the front seats, with the children's feet resting on them. The groceries had to be repacked into boxes for easier stacking. Finally, everything fit.

The weather report advised of an arctic front sweeping down the plains, so Cliff had Katja select sweat suits for herself and the children for the next day of travel, as well as the lighter weight windbreakers he had bought. That evening, the children were asleep by 8:30 PM with the adults being in bed shortly after the 10 PM news casts.

Sunday morning arrived early for Cliff and his new family. He was showered, shaved and dressed before 6:00 A.M. and in the motel office taking care of his bill just minutes later. As soon as the coffee had stopped brewing, at the self-serve breakfast bar, he filled his two thermos mugs and four juice glasses and was back in the room in time for the morning weather forecast.

Katja was up and getting dressed upon his return. He invited her to join him for their morning pick me up and an explanation of the forecast. They forecast an arctic front was sweeping down the plains toward Dallas. The temperatures were dropping and rain was expected in the DFW Metroplex within a short time. Ice should start forming in the area by noon.

They had to be away from here long before that. Snow and or ice was expected for the Wichita Falls area sometime during the early afternoon as a warm moisture laden gulf front moved north and collided with the cold air speeding south. Denver had freezing temperatures already. Snow was not expected for the panhandles of both Texas and Oklahoma until the morrow. They had to be home by then. They would be.

Together, they checked that everything was packed. While Cliff loaded the remaining items into the truck, Katja woke and dressed the children. Shortly after six thirty that morning they got under way.

The temperature was falling and the wind was gusting out of the north. Katja was glad Cliff had advised warmer clothing. The children where nodding off again, it was still dark outside. Traffic was heavy though, with rush hour in full swing, even on a Sunday. The Metro never rests.

Before setting off, Katja had refilled their coffee mugs and had made sure the children drank their juice. She had gotten them additional cups of juice and a couple of muffins each to hold them till Cliff would stop for something to eat. There was fruit and snacks available to them also.

Cliff had hoped to evade rush hour, thinking they were driving in the opposite direction of the majority of traffic, but that was not the case. The temperature was in the upper thirties and a fine mist was falling making for hazardous roads, as water mixed with oil covered roadways. Just after eight that morning, they had finally reached the northern section of Interstate 35W, just north of Fort Worth, just before the turn off to US 287 towards Wichita Falls and Amarillo. He drove directly into the wind.

When little Irina asked to use the toilet, Cliff stopped at the McDonalds in Decatur. He picked up breakfast to go at the same time. Once they got on the road again, the misting had stopped, although the wind continued, making him fight the wheel.

Katja was watching the landscape, commenting on the lack of vegetation and trees. She was amazed at how sparsely the land was populated. Cliff caught a glimpse of wild turkey and pointed them out to Katja and the children. He flushed a covey of bobwhite quail on the road verge and drew admiring oohs. But what really excited the children was the small herd of white tailed deer grazing in a meadow along the highway.

They arrived in Wichita Falls long before

lunch. With the new elevated highway running through the city, he had the truck maneuvered in and out of town in record time. The wind remained a problem once leaving Wichita Falls, for now they had a side wind and the gusts had a tendency to move the vehicle into the left-hand lane. Cliff was glad that the highway was mostly divided and traffic relatively sparse.

The children were coloring in their books and quiet for the most part. To keep spirits up, he popped one of the children's CDs in to the player. Soon songs were filling the vehicle. Cliff was singing along with the choir to Old McDonald and all the animals on his farm and to the itsy-bitsy spider that went up that water spout. Katja and the children promptly got the idea and sang along with the refrain.

When a train met them going in the opposite direction, Cliff would blow the car horn and wave. Usually the train engineer would reciprocate and the children would waive to abandon. Cliff would lower the window so their frantic waiving could be appreciated by the train personnel. The cold blast of air entering the vehicle helped keep everyone awake.

They stopped in Childress for food and gas. In a very short time they were on the go again with lunches perched on laps. The children fell asleep for a long nap after lunch. Katja used the time to make a list of items they still needed to purchase. Cliff dictated some of the items. The huge quantities, which Cliff specified, were worrisome to Katja. She was concerned that Milk and Orange juice might spoil, if they bought them it in the quantities Cliff requested. He tried to reassure her.

"We have a big side by side and a big freezer and another fridge in the utility room. Don't worry so, everything will fit."

To make the time fly faster, Cliff told Katja some of the history of the area. He talked of the importance of Palo Duro canyon, not so far away, to the Native Americans. Of the slaughter of their dietary staple, the buffalo, and of the significance of Fort Sill, just across the border in Oklahoma. He told of Geronimo and Cynthia Ann Parker and her son Quanah. He talked of the Texas Rangers of old, not the new service that Sasha admired so much, of the military forts that had once doted the region. He told of the Santa Rosa Round Up and of the Waggoner ranches in this area.

When they crossed the Prairie dog town branch of the Red River, he told her of the river's importance to the area. Katja was very surprised that such a fabled and important river should be dry. She thought, with just a little caution, one could cross it on foot. That there was no need for the enormous bridge, she had glimpsed, that spans the river bed.

"You should see that dry river during the rainy season or during snow melt up in the Rockies. It's a major river then and flooding of the roads occurs regularly."

Shortly after leaving Childress the chorus of "are we there yet?" commenced. Katja tried to keep the children occupied and told them to look out for bears. That surprised Cliff totally. He could not imagine where she had learned that phrase. He had to ask. At first, Katja did not comprehend the question, then she smiled, and repeated and rephrased the remark.

"Police are sometimes called bear? Especially when they check the speed of cars from a small plane? How interesting. No", she said, "I meant the animals. Sasha and Rina were looking for bears and wolves the whole time we were on the train in Siberia, all the way from our village to Yekaterinburg. Do you have bear and wolf here?" She wanted to know.

"Not here, but up in the mountains are black bear and perhaps some grizzly in Glacier National Park. No, not here. There are very few wolves left in the States, only at a few protected places. Not here. But we do have lots of his little brother, the coyote. We might see some. We definitively have those on the ranch."

"Is dangerous, that coyote?"

"Not so much to people, but my calves have at times been attacked by them. They also don't mind a foal every now and then. Coyote are very smart.

They know that there is refuse where people are, and they go through the trash if you let them. We have Snowball who keeps the area around the house and barns pretty well free of coyote."

"What is this snowball, some sort of device? I thought ball is made from snow, to throw at something."

"No, Snowball is my big white Great Pyrenees dog."

"Papi, you have dog? Can I play with it?"

"Rina, you don't know if the dog does bite. You might best stay away from it. Remember Oleg's dog is very fierce." Her brother reminded her.

There ensued a small battle between brother and Sister, with Rina insisting that her Papi could only have a good and gentle dog. The children had reverted to Russian in their frustration and their mother now intervened.

"I am sure that this Snowball is not a menace to your well-being. You must remember, however, that it is a farm dog and as such he has some duties that require him to be protective or fierce, whatever the situation calls for. If Mr. Cliff allows you to pet him, then I expect nothing but complete gentleness from my children when petting that animal. I am sure, that after you are introduced to the animal and he

134

becomes familiar with you, you have nothing to worry about."

Cliff did understand most of what Katja told the children and he promised to introduce them. He felt Snowball did not have a mean bone in his body, other than his complete annoyance with the wily coyote.

Their drive towards Amarillo continued. They had reached some sort of a plateau. The climbing had leveled off. Katja expected to see mountains in the distance, but she was disappointed when all she could glimpse where ugly, tall silos. Her inquiry as to their purpose yielded the information, that those where grain storage devises. She was also quite interested in the enormous fields, that looked as if something white had been spilled. When she asked about it, she was told. that the farmers where finishing the cotton harvest and the wagons with the wire cages full of white stuff, where filled with harvested raw cotton, on the way to a cotton gin to be cleaned and baled.

The children alerted him to a little girl playing with some sort of animal. Neither Katja nor the children could ascertain what kind of animal she was playing with. It was too small to be a horse, although the child was placing a big toy bear on the animals back and happily running with the beast. It could not be a sheep, nor a goat. The conformation was all wrong, although there was long wavy hair. Cliff swung off the highway and into the drive of the lonely farm house. He lowered the window and was just about to explain something, when the beast turned into a ferocious dog charging their vehicle. The little girl started crying, and a woman came out of the house.

"Can I help you?" she asked.

"I'm sorry 'ma'am. I did not mean to upset your little girl or your dog. Just wanted my family to see your dog. They've never seen a Pyrenees'. I've got one. I think they're the greatest dogs ever."

"Sugarbaby, come here. Them folks is okay. Come show off your stuff and let them kids pet you." Instantly the dog became docile. He jumped up on the car door, while Cliff scratched him behind the ears.

"Rina, you want to touch the dog, he's really very nice, see."

Tentatively, the little girl held her hand gingerly out of the window. The dog came over, sniffed her hand and then proceeded to lick her fingers. Rina was enchanted, but Sasha could not be enticed to touch the dog and he did not want to leave the safety of his vehicle. Katja was braver. She managed to pet the animals head and was surprised how soft his fur was. Cliff thanked the lady and heaved compliments upon the dog for his good behavior and his beautiful confirmation. Then he backed out of the yard and onto the highway once again.

"Brrr, but it is cold outside". Irina was shivering. Instantly the windows went up again. The car heater promptly provided a cozy warmth. It was just past midafternoon. A few tiny sporadic snowflakes kept hitting the windshield and then fluttered off. There was a sharp north wind whipping the bare branches of cottonwood and elm trees about. Tumbleweeds where climbing fences and raced across the highway, only to be snagged again on a fence on the opposite side of the road. It took only a few more minutes and highway 287 merged with Interstate 40. They had reached Amarillo.

Cliff made a B line to his favorite Albertson's Supermarket on the far side of town. His passengers were glad at the prospect of stretching their limbs. A bit of movement would be good. They also knew, that now they had finally reached the last leg of their almost two-week long journey. The excitement and anxiety that had plagued Katja through this whole endeavor was once again plaguing her.

Sasha too was quiet, while his old fears once again gnawed on his mind. Cliff too was thinking of home. He was sure Katja and the children would be happy there. But now the worries connected with the first real storm of the season troubled him. Only little Irina was totally content. She had no doubts what so ever. Her Papi would see to it, that everything about the new home, would be absolutely wonderful.

The steaks at Hofbrau's on I-40 in the western, newer section of Amarillo had been, as always, tender and tasty. Cliff had ordered a big steak for the children to share between them and French fries as well as a garden salad. For himself he'd ordered a baked potato with all the trimmings and Caesar salad, and a big T-bone steak. Katja opted for a filet mignon with burgundy mushrooms, a baked potato and a garden salad. They were all stuffed when they left the restaurant.

The last purchases where securely stowed away. The children were just about asleep in their seats. Katja too was sleepy. She could easily have nodded off, but a sense of commitment kept her awake. Cliff had been driving all day and the fatigue was telling around his eyes. She kept up a small chatter of inconsequential things, to keep him company.

The snow was getting heavier; the wind had not abated. In fact, it was driving the snow straight into the windshield and made visibility extremely difficult. It was dark now, moon and stars where hidden behind a thick layer of clouds. Traffic was minimal. The snow had by now covered the roadbed and driving was made all the more difficult because of the uniformity of the surface. The white and yellow road markings had been obliterated. Although Cliff knew this road well, he still drove hesitantly, for he did not wish to run off the highway and into a ditch.

It seemed to take forever to reach Dumas, where Cliff stopped at the Allsup's. Everyone got out for a pit stop. They all got hot drinks, chocolate for the children, cappuccino for the adults. It was bitterly cold. A driving wind had made the wind-chill to be somewhere near zero. Although the heater was going in the vehicle, it was still somewhat cold. Especially the floor. Of course, the children with their short legs, where not subjected to that discomfort.

Am I arriving in the Siberia of the United States? Katja was grousing to herself. She had gotten so used to the pleasant temperatures in Dallas. She had automatically assumed all of the United States of America had such temperate conditions in winter. Obverse, she did not realize that this blast of winter would not last for several months, as it would in Russia. They had not talked of that yet. There was so much to talk about. Most important was that they should get to know each other, what the other had experienced, to shape the personality and character of the person they had committed to.

She needed to make conversation. She realized that Cliff was having a hard time driving. If her chatter could help him in any way, she would. Cliff, too. realized that he needed to be engaged in something besides his driving. So, he asked Katja

"How did you ever wind up in Siberia. I

cannot imagine you doing anything so bad to be banished in Siberia."

"Oh, I was not punished, I was simply born there. But I had no way of getting out of there. Sergey, my husband, was send there after the Chernobyl nuclear disaster. He was a teenager then. He was send there, for he could not return to his home. Everything was so contaminated. They send him there for want of a better place. Him, and a bunch of other people.

The Gulag was still there, empty then. The government just used it, to relocate those displaced, helpless people. They arrived without anything. No clothing, no furniture, no pictures of the past, not even a toothbrush. Most of them died within a few years. They had all been contaminated in some way.

Sergey had been a little bit more lucky. He at least had been able to marry, have children and so be immortalized."

Katja was however worried about the children, especially Irina. Had Sergey transmitted in his genes, some of the altered chromosomes that had eventually killed him? She was not sure. She told Cliff of her concerns. He told her there was no sense in making herself sick with anxiety about something that might not have happened. To himself he promised that he would have the children checked, as soon as he had them adopted and covered by insurance.

"How did your family wind up in Siberia. Was your father and mother sent there by the Communists? Tell me what happened." She told him about her father's trip to the dacha.

"Papa arrived in late February of 1918. Ever since leaving that deserted estate, he had tried to avoid people. He had been so worried about crossing the Volga. There he would have to be amongst people and be under scrutiny. Luck was on his side.

"Somewhere west of the Volga, he really did not know where, he ran into a woman with her six children walking along the road, trying to stay away from the rabble. He gave them all a ride. The older boys rode his two mares, still tied to the sled. A girl and the youngest boy, he had on top of the hay, covered with horse blankets and the oldest girl with the baby, he had inside the cab. The mother rode with him on the seat and helped with the horses.

"Marina Marushkaya was trying to get to her husband somewhere near Sverdlovsk, that was the name the communists had given to the old Tsarist town of Yekaterinburg. She would send the children into towns, when they found them, to try to obtain food while the horses grazed along the verge of the road, where there was little snow. She told him that her husband was a peasant, who had supported the Bolsheviks and was now in command of a detachment. He had send for her and the children. She

141

could have taken the train, but somehow was uncomfortable with that. She had papers, which she gladly showed the many inspectors, but never showed him. He, however got glimpses of the documents several times and had to admit they looked as official as his, only something was wrong. The writing was not correct, it seemed to him illiterate scribble.

"Yet Marina was a good cover for him. He never had to show his papers, for she always included him with her children. The oldest son, taking care of the family, until they reached her husband.

"Whenever they were among people, Marina's language would become course, peasant like, and the children remained quiet. Once they had mastered the obstacle, she would converse with him and her children in very cultured Russian. She did not sound so very different from his mother. He could easily imagine her in fine clothing in charge of some estate in the Ukraine or Little Russia. But he did not dare to tell her what he suspected. He was afraid she would betray him to one of the roving bands of Bolsheviks. She and her children provided a wonderful cover for him when it came to cross the most important river in all of Russia. They had to go far to the north to finally find a bridge that they could cross.

"The commissars looked quite askance at them, but she had them convinced that this mother, with her seven children, was on her way to bring supplies and needed horses to her husband and his unit. So, they were allowed passage. She even managed to get bread and cheese and some milk to keep them all going for several days.

"Once they crossed the Volga, they started traveling in a more easterly direction. It took only a few more days and they reached the rail road tracks of the Trans-Siberian Train. Here Marina and the children left him. She would follow the tracks, and he would continue in a more northerly direction.

"Papa traveled for three more days until he found another secluded, deserted estate. There he rested the horses, saw to his equipment and packed additional supplies. He took what he needed, but all his life it bothered him, that he had stolen. By this time, he was unsure of what day, or even what month it was. He stayed until he felt rested enough to continue.

"Again, he stayed strictly to the back roads, at times even traveling across fields and meadows, across frozen ponds and through dense woods. It was deep Russian winter now. He dreaded having to cross the high mountains. However, the further east he traveled, the less he was bothered by the rabble or by Bolsheviks. He even was able to purchase food several times. Whenever he had the opportunity he bought as much as they would sell him. Where ever possible, he tried to replenish his feed and fodder for the animals.

"He was sure, his parents would never have recognized the stately troika or their once well-groomed son. He looked like the rabble he so tried to avoid.

"To avoid going into the mountains, Papa chose his route carefully. Eventually he had to go. When he was within walking distance of the first peaks he looked for another estate where he could rest his team and replenish all supplies. He found it in a small valley, curiously devoid of most snow. He also found two cows. They were hungry, but well and pregnant. To leave them behind might cause them to starve and he needed the milk they might eventually give. By this time, Nicolay had no illusions to what he might find or not find at the dacha. He knew he would most likely have to make it on his own.

"On a clear, sunny, bitter cold day, sometime in January, he headed up the slopes. The cows trudged behind the sled just like his extra horses. He even had found several chickens and a rooster. No, they were not laying, but they would in a couple of months.

"He took it slow. He never pushed the animals. They all moved at an alarmingly slow rate, but a save rate. Where the snow cover was not so deep, he allowed the animals to browse to save on feed. The higher up into the mountains they went, the steeper the slopes, the slower his progress. There were harrowing moments when snow slipped away under their feet. When the path was so narrow, it threatened to topple the troika. When the animals strained so hard and they did not budge the sled, he got out and pushed from behind himself, putting chocks under the back wheels to prevent the sled from slipping backwards. Still, he was afraid they would not make it. He persevered.

"Once he crested the range that divides Asia from Europe, the going became just a little easier. He saw no people. Only wild animals, and here and there in the valleys he found evidence of human activity. There were some abandoned hay stacks, he put to good use. He found deserted cabins, abandoned or just left for the season. He was not sure. But he used them as refuges for himself and his animals. On snowy days, he just kept in camp or cabin, wherever he was.

"When he finally arrived at his family's hunting estate, he was so tired, he gave no thought of reconnoitering, who was or was not there. He just drove up, unhitched his team and stabled them. There was feed and water in the stable, straw and hay. He released the chickens into the tack room, until he could manage better accommodations, and fell asleep on a hay stack.

"The animals woke him. There was no telling how long he had been asleep, but his stallion had gotten out of his stall and was nibbling his face. It was time to feed them all again. After that he looked around. A hot bath sounded marvelous, hot food even better.

"Papa had been prepared for the possibility that all their serfs and servants would be missing. To confront that certainty was very disheartening. He told me many times that if it had not been for the animals and his responsibly to them, he would have gone mad. He was alone for two years in that dacha and supported himself and the horses, cows and chickens with what he was able to grow and hunt.

"Twice a year, he had to make a journey to humanity. He needed some supplies: shoes, coffee, tea, seeds, sugar, soap. The first time he made the trip, he was able to use some of his rubles, but on the second trip, the money had become worthless. He was afraid to use the gold crowns he had or the *Theresien Taler.*

"He could not allow himself to become suspect. He brought items to barter: honey that he had been able to rob from some wild bees, clothes that he had outgrown and some of his families clothing left behind on visits to the dacha. He also had butter and cheese to sell and a few fresh vegetables.

"Papa lived in the most abject isolation, depending for his survival on his own skills and the companionship of his animals. During his first year there, he observed a pack of feral dogs and was able to entice one to stay with him. Dancer would be with him for almost twenty years, a remarkable agreement.

"The kitten he found on one of his excursions to the surrounding habitations became his loyal bedpartner, along with the dog. Even while he was living away from the dacha, the animals stayed with him in the gulag.

"During his third year at the dacha, an older couple moved into one of the empty huts in the village. Papa watched them for many days and found both to be industrious, trying to survive as best they could. Finally, my father found the courage to go see them. He liked them at first sight. They were struggling to collect and grow produce to get them through the winter months ahead.

"Papa made them an offer. He was so desperate for human voices, but he also knew that three pair of hands working together had a much better chance. And so, the couple moved into one of the rooms at the dacha. That building was much sturdier and able to keep the wind and cold out.

"Anouchka and Arkady moved into what had once been the family's dining room. There was a wood stove in that room. Papa moved into his father's library. He had two reasons to move into that room. It had all the books he loved to read, a stove and most of all, it had the hidden escape passage and access to the underground storage area where he had secreted all the family's precious belongings. He had even stored some of the better furniture down there.

"Anouchka took over the cooking, washing, dairy and preserving of food. Together they went to harvest mushrooms and berries. They also were able to fish and preserve the catch by smoking or freezing. It was a happy cooperation, for the skills Father lacked, the others seemed to have. Life continued this way until about 1929, when several families had moved into the abandoned village.

"Life continued to the rhythm of the seasons. With the help of his new partners, Father was able to bring in a much larger harvest of hay and grain to sustain the animals and humans comfortably till the next harvest. They were able to fell trees together and sell them as firewood further down the valley. All went well ..."

Rinnnggg... The cell phone in Cliff's pant pocket was going off.

"Katja, dear, please can you get it out of my pants? I hate to take my hands off the wheel." Katja obliged him. She gingerly slipped her hand into his right pocket and immediately felt the phone. Flipping the phone open, she held it to Cliff's ear. After Cliff identified himself, he listened intently for a few second and then gave instructions in a clipped voice. He also informed the caller of his present location. The last thing he said was; "It would be good to have the snowplow waiting for us at the State line."

A caravan consisting of a snow plow, several trucks and cars, including the SUV carrying the Collins family arrived in Boise City a few minutes after 11:00 P.M. Sheriff Don Brewer was waiting for them at the courthouse square. Most were local folks the sheriff allowed to go home. A couple of travelers were invited to spend the night in the one local motel. Others, the sheriff advised, to spend the night with kinfolks in town.

For his friend, Cliff Collins and family, he had other plans. First, he invited the family to stay with him. Don knew Cliff would nix that proposal, and so he sent the Navigator with his blessing on toward the ranch in the company of a sheriff's officer's patrol vehicle and the snow plow. The last thing Don said was: "Take it easy, Cliff. You know the way. If you need me, I'll be at the house. I've told the guys to call it a night when they have you safely at the ranch. Jorge has been scraping the ranch road and is waiting for you at the county road."

Then he turned to Katja. "I'm sorry, Ma'am, we could not give y'all a better welcome. It was planned, you know. You must think you came into Siberia again. But I have it on good authority, this stuff will be gone by tomorrow afternoon. Donna and I will come by later tomorrow, when the road is better. Take care now y'all and have a good night."

They continued on to their destination in the deteriorating road conditions. It took much longer than expected. If it had not been for the snow plow and the sheriff's SUV, they would have had a much harder time. Finally, shortly before midnight, Cliff pulled off the highway.

True to his word, Jorge was waiting at the gate post to the ranch. They followed a very bumpy path past some buildings. An older home was on their left and a few yards later, a barn and out- buildings. *This must be part of the ranch,* Katja thought, but she could not see their home. From what Cliff had told her, it dominated the surrounding ranch and could be seen from the highway. She tried to strain her eyes, looking through the swirling snow. She knew from experience that everything would be obscured in such a blizzard.

And then, faintly, she could ascertain a light in the distance. It became more brilliant, or maybe there were several lights? Cliff slowed down. Jorge on his tractor turned off the path, waved and then turned around.

Chapter Six

We're here, Sweetheart. I know you can't see the house because of this snow, but we're home." Suddenly, the road improved to smooth rolling while, at the same time, Cliff braked the vehicle to a halt. He had stopped in front of some huge doors, protected from the snow.

"We're finally home, you all. Sorry it took so long, and was such a scary ride. Tomorrow, things'll look better. Are you all ready to get out?"

"Mama, we don't have any shoes on. How far do we have to walk?"

"I don't know, Sasha, but you better put on your shoes and coats. Just in case."

"Mr. Cliff, is it far from here or should we just carry the children?"

"It's not far, but they better put on their shoes. I know it's inconsiderate on my part, but I've been hoping all evening that you all would come into the house through the front door the first time, else I could just let the garage doors up, and we'd be in the house. Do you mind taking about twenty extra steps?"

"That is not far, but I don't see the house, just this big door. What is it?"

"The garages. The house is around that side. Come, you will see. I just wish it wasn't snowing so bad." With that, Cliff climbed out of the vehicle and came around to open the passenger doors.

"Brrr, it's cold. Come! Do you kids have your shoes on?"

"Not yet, almost."

"Well, follow us when you're ready."

Clifford guided Katja around the corner to the front of the house. Lights were blazing. Here, in the protection from wind and snow, Katja could see that it was a big house, maybe bigger than the dacha back home. It looked warm, inviting and substantial, just like on the picture he had sent her.

There was a big, covered front porch with a swing on one end and a couple of rocking chairs and at the other end a settee, two chairs and a low table. The furniture was made of a dark rattan with colorful cushions on which to sit. Everything looked so inviting. Katja recognized the scene from the picture that had been sent to her. A glass door and a big wooden door behind it led into the house. Cliff was now fumbling with his keys to open it.

At just that moment, Irina came flying up onto the porch.

"A kitty, Mama! Look, a kitty!" She started petting the animal instantly, sitting on the cold concrete floor.

"Come, Katja, let me carry you over the threshold. It's the custom. The groom carries his bride for the first time into the house. I think we qualify." He bent down and picked up Katja with both arms. She wrapped hers around his neck, and so she entered her new home.

The last glimpse of her daughter was that the little girl was trying to manhandle the cat into the house. Irina was too small to carry that big animal, and so she just held the upper half of the animal and the legs were trying to walk with the little one towards the door.

Aleksandr's attention too was captivated by a

large animal. A big, white dog was staring at him, sitting down, his eyes locked with the boys. The animal looked very much like that ferocious beast, they met earlier in the day, but this dog had a much kinder demeanor and expression about his face. Then, Katja was inside the house.

Cliff was saying, "Welcome home, Katja. I do hope you like it here."

Then he put her down gently. She was standing in some sort of entrance hall, not really a vestibule. There was no door that closed it off from the apartment and made the space private from the other inhabitants. She was standing on tile, and above her, a chandelier glittered that would have done the residence in St. Petersburg proud. Someone had fastened a sprig of something green with white berries to it. Cliff saw it, too.

"Well, it's custom too. I have to kiss you now. Whenever a female is caught under a sprig of mistletoe, we men are given the job of kissing her. Especially if that female is as fetching as you are." He bent down, cupping her face in his hands and gently, at first, gave her a kiss on the lips. As it registered that she was responding, he reciprocated by kissing more urgently. "If I continue with this, I know where we're going to end up. Look around a bit. To your right is the library and the stairs to the upstairs rooms. In front of you is the family, great room, living room, whatever you are going to call it. To your left is the dining room. I'm going to get the kids in.

"Papi, is it okay if the kitty sleeps with me?"

"If that is what Princess wants, it's okay with me. You might want to ask Mama for permission. Here, let me help you." Cliff picked up the cat with one hand, and with the other he carried the little girl into the house and to her room. "Here you are. Do you like your room?"

"This is my room? But it's a princess room. I'm not a princess. Oh, I can sleep here?" Rina was almost speechless.

"Yes, you sleep here, and play too, if you want, and Princess likes sleeping on your bed."

"Who is Princess?"

"The cat, the one you wanted to sleep with you. See, she is on your covers already."

"Papi, I got to go. Can you show me the toilet?"

"It's right there. Sasha and you will have to share. His room is right through here, see."

"Does he have to come through my room to get to his?"

"No, there is another door from the hall."

"Where is the seat, Papi?"

"It's right there. Do you need help with that?"

"No, I'm a big girl, Papi." How could her darling Papi have forgotten that? He must be dreadfully tired.

"Okay, then I'll see after Sasha and Mami."

Mami was standing still in the front hall, slowly turning in circles. Tears were running down her cheeks and having the biggest smile he had seen on her. She kept whispering something in Russian that Cliff did not understand. She was mesmerized. Her one arm was stretched out at whatever she was looking and the other clasped in disbelieve across her face.

Sasha was just being herded into the house by Snowball. The dog had understood that it was too cold outside for the child. He had taken one of Sasha's sleeves into his mouth and pulled him gently towards the door.

Aleksandr himself had a most disbelieving smile on his face. There was wonderment in his voice as he told Cliff, "He likes me, he likes me! He made me pet him, scooping up my hand with his muzzle and then tipping his head up so my hand will slide across his head. I wasn't scared at all Mr. Cliff. Where is the bathroom? I need to go, please."

"Irina is using yours, but there is the powder room right here." He opened the door.

"Is that all right, Sasha?"

"Yes, thank you."

Sasha was sitting on the throne thinking this was one odd bathroom. It was nicely done, better than at the hotel. There were nice colorful towels and pictures on the wall and a little basket with some magazines. The sink was in a cabinet with a huge mirror above it and little lights on either side. There was a full roll of the softest tissue paper he had ever used, better even than in the hotel, by far softer than the old newspaper they had used at the dacha.

Something was missing, though. Then he figured it out. There was no tub. No shower either. Yet it was big enough so one could wash oneself from head to toe. Only he'd hoped that there would be a tub in which he could submerge himself. That would have been fun. Well, Mr. Collins had fibbed a little. He could not fault the man. The house, what he had seen of it, was very nice indeed. The boy could hear his sister prattling outside his door. *God, what is she so excited about? She can always only see the most fabulous things in life, and here, clearly, was a bit of disappointment. Aleksandr flushed and washed his hands. Well, at least that worked.*

As Sasha exited the bathroom, he found his sister urgently tugging on his mother's hand.

"Mama, come, you must see my bed room. It is so gorgeous. Just for a princess ballerina, come see. Come, Mami, come. Sasha and I have our own bathroom." She was chattering on and on. Cliff was there too and the dog.

"Are you ready to find your own room?"

Probably the size of a shoebox the boy thought. It just could not all be fabulous, like his sister always thought. *Well, here goes.* The child followed Cliff through part of a very big room, which Cliff called a family room and then through a smaller eating area, which he called the breakfast area and down a long hallway. There were doors to either side. Irina was just pulling their mother into the first door on the right.

"It's down here, Sasha, the last door in this hall. Come see, I hope you like it. I'm sorry, you and Irina will have to share a bathroom. It connects your rooms. If it makes you feel better, you can always keep the connecting doors open."

Aleksandr stood there for a moment, immobile. The room looked like what he imagined a cowboy might have for his room. He looked for the toilet and the tub in the bathroom, but could not find either.

"Is there a tub and a seat?" He asked tentatively.

"Sure, right through here." For a long time, the boy just stood there looking, then he went back into his room. Over the bed, there was a big Ranger star, and his bed cover looked like jeans, with a cowboy swinging a lasso on it. Snowball nuzzled his hand. Sasha was not feeling it. Big, wet tears were running down his face. It was too much to fathom. Cliff did not notice the tears. Rina had come and once again hugged his knees.

"Papi, you're the best." In the same breath, she called out, "Mama, come see Sasha's room."

Katja trailed after her.

"Oh, my, how wonderful. Do you like it Sasha?"

Cliff looked at the little boy then waiting for his response to his mother's question.

"Sasha, what's wrong? Why are you crying? Don't you like the room, we fixed it especially for you? If you don't like it, we can change it."

The boy only started crying harder. "Oh, I'm

so bad, Mama. Mr. Collins is not going to like me at all. I'm so bad, so very bad."

"Sasha, I don't think you're bad at all. Did you do something wrong we don't know about? If you did, tell us, so we can correct it. I just can't imagine you doing anything wrong or bad. You're just about the most wonderful boy I ever met." Cliff tried to console the child.

"Mama, tell him I'm bad. I'm so sorry." He sniffled harder.

"Sasha, I don't know what you did, and Mr. Cliff does not know either, it seems. So why don't you tell us what you did, and then we decide what kind of punishment you need. But don't cry anymore."

"You know, Mama, Oleg told me, I have to be the man of the family now and protect you and Rina. He said so. He said that if things weren't good here, we would go back to Russia and be with our friends at home. It's just that Mr. Collins is so nice. There has not been anything to go to Russia again for. Everything is so much nicer. I got more toys, clothes and books than ever before. And now this room. No boy has ever had such a room. I can tell Sergey about it. He won't believe it." Here he sniffled some more.

"I've been hoping that something is not as Mr. Collins says. That something is bad, but it never is. I so want to play with Sergey again and have Oleg to talk to. Now it's never going to be." There was another rush of tears. "When Mr. Collins just now took me to the bathroom, I finally thought I'd found something not so good. You know, there is no bathtub or shower in that bathroom, and I thought even the bathroom in the hotel is better. So now maybe we find more stuff not so good and get to go home again.

But then he showed me our bathroom, and it's so much better than any bathroom I ever have ever seen. I'm so bad. I not believe Mr. Collins, and I wish for bad stuff, so we can go back to Russia. Now, he will never like me." The tears just rushed down his cheeks. The boy was overwrought.

"Sasha," Cliff got down on his knee, so he could look right at the boy's face, to be even with him. "Sasha, you did nothing wrong, and you are not bad. Everybody has thoughts like that. I was wondering about you, when I was on my way to pick you up. I was worried, you would not like me. Or that your Mama did not want to come. I did not know you were on the train so long. When I called the hotel in Moscow, and you were not there, I thought you would not come at all.

"I thought that maybe you children might be ill-behaved. Or would not listen to me. So many dreadful things went through my mind. That is what's called worrying. Big people do that a lot. I'm sure your Mama had the same thoughts. It's part of being a grown up.

162

"That you want to see your friends again is only normal. I want to see my friends too. I am lucky, most of them live around here. Sasha, I promise you, you will see your friends again. I don't know when. I know it will be a long time from now. It depends on so many grown up things. If we can't go and visit, perhaps they can visit us. Would you like that?" The boy nodded shyly, disbelievingly, but still hopeful. Cliff continued.

"Sasha, you are the most well-behaved boy I know and so responsible. You try to look after Irina and your Mama. It is wonderful that you want to help. It's also my job from now on, but I'll appreciate all the help you give me. Is that a deal, partner? Shake on it." Cliff Collins put his big hand out, and the child placed his little one in it. They shook solemnly. There was still one more thing he had to explain to the child.

"There is a good reason, why there is no tub or shower in that little bathroom. It's for company, who do not spend the night. There is no reason to have a tub. You know, sometimes people come by for just a little while. Some of them we don't even know so well. Sometimes, someone may be a little sick, having a cold or some such thing. We would not want them to spread their germs around to our bathrooms for us to pick up. The little bathroom is just fine and easily cleaned afterward. Do you understand what I am saying?"

"Da, Mr. Cliff. I think so."

Aleksandr wanted to talk more. His mother, however, cut in.

"Sasha, I think it is time for you to go to bed tonight. It is very late, and we are tired too, but we still have to bring all our things in from the truck and put them away. We can talk and explore in the morning. Now, get ready for bed. You too, Irina."

"Sleep good, you two," Cliff said as he was leaving the room and to Katja, "I'm going to pull the vehicle into the garage and start bringing in the perishables. I'm afraid we'll have to put them up tonight."

"I'll be there as soon as I tuck them in," Katja confirmed.

"But we don't have any sleepers here. We can't go to bed yet." Irina was whining.

Cliff called back. "There is one pair for each in the closets."

How sweet that man is. He thought of everything. I am so lucky. Katja was grateful; for his thoughtfulness. Her little daughter had a more practical question.

"What's a closet, Mama?"

"I don't know, Rina, but we shall find out.

Come!"

"No, let's ask my Papi."

Her mother, however, had already turned into the little girl's bedroom. She looked turning in a circle. What was behind those doors? Katja opened them, and there on a shelf was a pretty, pink nightgown for her daughter.

"Here, Rina, your papi thought of everything. Now, I better check on Sasha. You get ready for bed, young lady." She found the closet right away, and there too, were night clothes for her son. Handing them to the boy, who was already partially undressed, she told him she had seen toothbrushes and paste in the bathroom. She admonished both her children not to forget to brush. She would be back in a minute to tuck them in.

Rina had to have the last word. "Papi needs to kiss us good night, too. Don't forget."

Katja almost bumped into Cliff as he came in from the garage laden with two heavy sacks. She helped him, taking one of the sacks and carrying it to the kitchen. She started to put things away into the refrigerator. The size of that appliance was astonishing to Katja. Cliff had told her to put only one of each item into the kitchen refrigerator on the way home from Amarillo and advised they would put additional items into the back-up appliances in the utility room.

Until a few moments ago, she had no idea what a utility room was. Now she knew that was where clothes would be washed and folded and ironed. Here, in this rather small room, were three more large appliances to keep foods frozen or cold.

She knew of none in her village in Russia who had one such appliance. Perhaps, big city restaurants had such magnificent coolers, but a home would never be equipped with such a lavish device. You just put items that needed to be kept cold on the window sill, inside in winter, outside in summer. You went shopping for food on your way home from work every day.

Cliff had told her they would go and do the major shopping once a month, and he would pick up milk, bread and perishables in town every so often, as needed. It was a totally foreign concept to shop for several weeks of groceries at one time. Katja realized, she had a lot to learn.

It took only a few minutes to stow away all the perishable foods. That surprised Katja also. It had taken such a long time to assemble the items. Cliff even brought in boxes with breakfast foods, and of course, all the fruits and vegetables. He was afraid they might freeze outside and so become inedible. When they had the most urgent food items stored, Cliff asked what was urgent that she have in the house as far as clothing was concerned. After that he opened the bottle of champagne that had been cooling in the fridge.

"Come, let's toast your arrival in your new home. Have you had a chance to look around yet?"

"I've seen the children's rooms and the rooms there at the front of the house and the utily room. Is that right? We not have such a space in Russia. Washing is done in kitchen for little things or for big in basement washroom. I have just one question. How many families live in this house, and with how many women must I share the kitchen and the utily room?"

"I don't understand your question. This is our house. We live here. No other people live here."

"But it is so big. Surely other people share this huge house with us."

"No, no one lives here but the four of us. Until now, I was the only one to live here. This is a one family home. Let me show you, and you will see that it is only our home."

"This house is so big. In Russia, several families would live in a home this size."

"Come, let's have a look around." He refilled the flutes. "You know the kitchen pretty well, but let me show you what is here. By the way, I want you to

arrange the kitchen to your liking. What is here is
what an old bachelor has found handy, and what the
cleaning woman tried to keep in order. You arrange
the cupboards to your liking. Okay?"

"Da, what is cupboards?"

"Those cabinets over the counters and below.
This is the pantry, where most of our food is kept, that
is, the stuff that does not need to be refrigerated. Most
foods go into the fridge, once they have been opened.
See here. Here in the pantry, there are spaces for the
kid's cereal and the soft drinks and juices. There is a
space for oils and canned vegetables or fruit. You can
arrange that how best it suits you. Here under the
cooktop, we keep some of the pots and pans, and the
lids go on these racks on the door.

"Our trash goes here under the sink. I've kept
most cleaning things right here, but you might want
to change that, so the kids can't get to them. Most are
bad for them, you know. The most often used small
appliances are here in the appliance garage. This shelf
pulls down, so you can put your cookbook here, while
you work. Cups and glasses are on this shelf and
plates and bowls are here. I think you 'll figure it out.
Just open doors 'till you find what you need. It's your
house now, after all."

"Da, too tired now to remember. Let's just go
see."

"Good idea, Sweets." Cliff was still trying out names for her. So, they wandered through the house, Cliff opening all doors and telling her what was behind them. She was amazed by the size of the garage. Katja had expected the garage to be almost empty, except for the Navigator. That vehicle was in the garage, but there on the far side of the space was another vehicle, one of the almost ubiquitous small trucks called a pick-up truck.

She was totally astounded that Cliff should have another vehicle, and that they should be parked inside the building. She confided, that at home people who had cars put them into old barns or left them out beside the house, covering the hood with old blankets. Not too many people had cars in her village. If you needed to go someplace, you took the train or bus.

He told her that the garage doubled as storage space for many people, because houses just did not have basements anymore. He also showed her the door that went down to the storm shelter.

"Oh, is basement to store potatoes and coal for heating? That is good, yes?" And after taking a peek down there she was surprised that it was empty: only a couple of chairs, a metal cabinet and a few little water bottles, a radio and flashlight. "Why you not store fuel down there for furnace?"

"This is not a basement, Sweets. It's a storm shelter, for when a tornado comes and we must hide from the wind."

"Please explain, this tomato? I thought tomato is vegetable you eat."

"You're right, a tomato we can eat or grow in our garden. A tornado is a wind that is very bad. It usually comes in a thunderstorm. It will destroy most anything in its way. That is what we need a shelter for."

"I know something like a shelter from bombs or from the stuff that bombs rain on us."

"Not really. I suppose you could use it for that. But you do not spend a long time in a storm shelter. Just a few minutes, when the storm has passed, you can come out again. It is just for some especially bad weather. Does that make sense to you?"

"Maybe, I too tired to think now. This bad storm, it comes every day?"

"No, no, I'll explain another day. Don't worry about it now. Let me show you our home."

He showed her the library and the dining room and then the upstairs. He confided that he had used Irina's new bedroom as his office but now he had taken a corner of the upstairs playroom as his office. Would she please impress on the children not to play with his papers and his computer? Yes, she would.

But they would never do such a thing in the first place. Her children did not touch things that were not theirs. She assured him.

She was amazed at the pool table. How would anyone ever believe her, when she told them, there was a pool table in the house. There was a pool table in the village. It had appeared in the first bar that opened after the fall of Communism. But in a house? Ah, yes, in the old days, there may have been a pool table at the dacha.

"So, people come to play pool here and drink vodka and you make lots of money from that. Like the bar in the village at home?"

He did not understand her. "Maybe you and I can play some pool when the weather is too bad to be outside. I play with my friend Don, who is the sheriff you met, and sometimes some of my other friends, but this is not a bar. However, we may have a drink or a beer while we play and sometimes we watch football games and play pool. But I don't charge my friends to play and strangers are not allowed in here. Do you understand what I'm saying?"

"I think so. Pool table is just for friends, yes?"

"Yes."

There was a very comfortable bedroom upstairs, with its own bath and a closet. Cliff showed her the attic storage.

"What is big black machine making so much noise?" She wanted to know.

"It's the heating unit," she was told.

"Not big stove heat house?"

"No, it's this big electric unit that keeps us warm. You set the thermostat and the unit delivers the heat to each area as you want it. I usually keep the upstairs a little cooler in winter because I'm never up here. But now things are changing. I usually keep the bedrooms cooler too, because that's good for sleeping. Again, with the children, you have to tell me what they like or set the temp to your liking."

They went downstairs again, with Cliff pointing out the coat closet and the guest bath. He refilled their glasses with the last of the champagne, and then, with his arm around Katja, he pointed the way to the master suite. Katja's breath escaped audibly as she entered the large, airy bedroom. Even in the middle of the night, the feeling of space and light was unmistakable. The bed dominated the room. To her left, a large dresser with a three-way mirror occupied the wall. There were windows to either side of the bed and at the far wall was a cozy sitting area with a big comfortable chair and a small chaise to either side of a round table. The sitting area was perfect for an afternoon rest or the first cup of coffee of the day. There was a book next to the big chair and a magazine rack on the other side. A table lamp illuminated the area.

The last wall held a huge wardrobe of the kind they had in Russia. Only this one had several drawers from the middle down. The top doors were closed. *Perhaps that is where cliff stores his shirts and jeans,* Katja thought, *but where am I to keep my things? He bought me so much. It will never all fit into this small wardrobe.*

"It's a good thing the little bathroom is so close by. We won't have to run so far, if we have to go in the middle of the night," she said approvingly.

"No, no, Sweetheart. Our bathroom is right there, and he opened a door on her right and walked her into a space filled with glass and mirrors. Everything sparkled. There were two washbasins connected and surrounded by a huge slab of highly polished marble, topped by the biggest mirror she had ever seen, bigger even than the one in the hotel. To her left, there was the biggest tub imaginable. Not even Hollywood films had shown her a bathroom such as this. Near the rear was another area enclosed by glass and tiled.

"What is that, please tell me."

"Our shower. I like to have a shower in the mornings to wake me up and I like a good, hot bath with the jets pummeling me, to massage sore muscles at night."

"Oh, but where is the toilet, or is that what the little bath is for?"

"No, Sweets, it's right here." He opened a door she had overlooked on the left.

"Do you like the bathroom?"

"Oh yes, I've never seen anything like it. There were some pictures like this in the magazines Deena showed me, but I could not imagine that such a thing really exists."

"Back here is our dressing room and walk in closet. See. I've left you all these hangers so you can put up your things. The drawers here are for you, too, and these shelves for sweaters and T-shirts. This is a shoe rack. I had no idea how many shoes you have, so I had them design the closet as most American women would like it, but if you need to make the space a little different, we can reconfigure this easily. Some of these components just snap in and can be replaced by shelves or hanging space."

"I don't have so many clothes. Everything will fit in just that little space there. You can spread out your things more."

"Oh, I have plenty. I'm sure as you acquire

your summer wardrobe, you will fill this all up." *More clothes*? Katja could not imagine. But she said nothing.

She was happy though, such a home as this, as was hers now, she could never have imagined in Russia. Spontaneously she turned to Cliff and hugged and kissed him passionately. He wrapped his arms around her and responded with just as much fervor, his hands exploring her back, hair, and finally pressing her body to his. Katja, too, let her fingers trace his body. They were both so tired, and happy and the alcohol had removed the inhibitions, they had imposed upon themselves. They let nature take over.

It was close to 3:00 A.M. when they fell asleep exhausted. Cliff was asleep before Katja had even had a chance to adjust pillows and blankets to her comfort. They woke late the next morning by Cliff's standards. Katja's sleep rhythm had been so disturbed over the past couple of weeks that she did not know whether it was morning or afternoon. She asked him what day it was and what time.

"It's almost eight. Yikes! I have to get going. I'll make us coffee and see if the kids are still down." He padded out of the room. She heard a door open and close, and a second later, Snowball was charging past the bedroom windows with Princess in close pursuit. She got up found the Turkish cloth robe he had told her last night was hers and turned the shower on. By the time Cliff returned to the bedroom, she was toweling her hair dry.

He told her the children were still sleeping, but he expected them to wake soon. He'd let the animals out; they too would want to come back in soon. Over coffee, he told her what he needed to do this morning. There was the stock to see to; he'd probably break the ice on the ponds and watering troughs. Jorge, Inez' husband, was most likely already feeding.

She would be over soon to help Katja in the house. Katja told him she thought she was going to be fine alone with the children. They could explore their new surroundings and get comfortable with the place. She would finish unloading the vehicle with their help. Cliff told her he would also have to go to town to check on county business and make sure no travelers were stranded and that the roads where passable. He expected to be home again for a late lunch. Would she make them something or should he pick up some food in town?

They dressed hastily, she in the sweats from yesterday. Then she prepared eggs, bacon and toast for breakfast. Irina was the first to join them. She came and gave her mother a morning hug and kiss, and then she hopped onto Cliff's lap for a taste of his breakfast. Aleksandr came stumbling from his room looking for the dog. He smelled the food and was instantly ravenous.

"I should be home for lunch about 1:00 o'clock. If I am delayed, I'll call you and let you know. Okay?"

"Yes, of course. But where is the telephone and what is your number?"

"Right there in that caddy. You can take it with you throughout the house. My number is in memory. Hit memory two." She looked at him, puzzled.

"See here. Watch me." He showed her and his phone started ringing. She looked even more befuddled, and he explained. "I called myself, Katja. Here let me call the house phone so you know the sound of the ringer."

"Papi, don't go!"

"I have to, Sweets."

"I want to come, please."

"I think you should stay home with me and help me cook lunch and dinner for your Papi. How is that, Irina?"

"But I want to go with Papi."

"Rina, it's very cold outside and Papi wants to hurry back home. You would just make it harder for

177

him. So, help me take care of things here. I really need you. You can help Sasha put his clothes up, and me, and then put your things up too. See how much a help you can be for me?"

"Okay" came the dejected answer. "But Papi, I need a hug and kiss before you go. And Mami too."

Cliff laughed. "That, I can do with pleasure." He picked up Irina and gave her a big smooch on the cheek. Katja's hug was much more intimate, and so was her kiss. "Call me if you need anything. Okay?"

"I want to come along and help you." Sasha swallowed his last bite. Cliff however had learned a quick lesson from Katja.

"If you really want to help me, Son, would you help your mother clean out the car? You would be a huge help for me. I would not have to worry about her working so hard. Also, if there is any problem, call me. See here. You push this button, and then that one, and I'll answer." He affectionally ruffled the boy's hair and was out the door.

Katja and the children sat for a little while over another cup of tea. The conversation centered about all the wonders of their new home. Rina offered her mother her own bedroom, so she would not have to sleep on the couch and offered to share Sasha's room with him.

"Don't you like your ballerina bedroom?"

"Oh, Mami, I love it. But I want you to have your own bed too, and not have to sleep on the couch or on the floor like Tatiana Bukhachev sometimes must."

"I have my own bed, Rina, but you have not seen the whole house yet. It was so late last night. Come you two, let's have a look."

"There is more? Mr. Cliff must be very rich." Sasha was totally surprised. So Katja took her children to the master suite. While there, she straightened up the bed and put the few clothes lying about where they belonged. The animals too were standing by the door, wanting in again. Sasha expressed his surprise at the size of the bed.

"It's as big as a room. We can all fit into that."

Rina however had discovered the tub. "Mami, can we swim in that?"

"I suppose you could, sometimes. Mr. Cliff says it's lots of fun."

"What is that glass room for, Mama?" Sasha wanted to know.

"It's a shower like we had in the hotel in the tub. That looks like fun too."

"Mami, there is no poty. You can use ours." Rina was finding all the missing things.

"There is one, in this little cubby. See?"

"Mama, where do you put your clothes? There is no wardrobe here." Aleksandr too was now observant.

"This little room back here, see."

"Mama, that is bigger than Sergey and Elena's bedroom at home."

"Guys, you have to start thinking of this as our home. We don't know it as well as the dacha yet, but we will soon. Just appreciate how big and wonderful this new home is." With that she took her brood upstairs to show them what was up there and asked them not to touch anything on Papi's desk. She stressed that.

"You know, Rina, he gave up his office so you could have your ballerina bedroom. Was that not thoughtful of him? Now, we have to be thoughtful of his things, also."

"Why does he have to have an office? I thought he was a farmer, working outside with the animals all the time?" Sasha was curious.

"Well, I don't know exactly. I guess he must

keep records of all sorts of things. He was also talking of working for the county. Some sort of political job. I really don't understand everything yet. Last night, when we were driving home, he got a few phone calls and made some decisions. I will have to learn more. But he was very concerned with the welfare of people. I just can't understand, why such a little bit of snow should cause such consternation. Maybe things are different here.

"Come let's go down and get started on our chores."

They unloaded the vehicle. Little Irina was steadfastly toting large bags into the house. She had gotten the message that her things went into her bedroom and Sasha's things into his. Sasha was carrying the larger bags into the house. The really heavy stuff, like the groceries, Katja brought in herself.

In order to find her way through the kitchen, Katja opened all doors and had a good look around. For the time being, she would keep things the way they were. No sense having everyone in the house lost.

She started emptying boxes and bags. It was amazing to her how everything fit. In no time at all most of the food items were stored away. Lunch would be coming up soon. On a cold day like this, a good, hearty soup would be welcome and a few slices of that nice dark bread she had found in Dallas. She found the roast she had left out of the freezer and cut a few chunks off that to start her soup. While the meat cooked, she cleaned and chopped up vegetables. She sautéed them, then added that to the meat and stock. At last, she added a portion from a big head of cabbage and diced potatoes to the pot.

She let the soup simmer while she helped Irina arrange her clothes and toys in her room. Sasha was already arranging his things on hangers and shelves. When she looked up to check on her food, it was close to noon, and she still had not started on her own things, nor had she started washing their clothes. She added thyme and rosemarie, garlic, a bit of pepper for seasoning and a small can of diced tomatoes to the pot. A handful of frozen corn would be good too and something to thicken the soup, a grain of sorts. Maybe a handful of groats. She had purchased a package, with just such a meal in mind.

The telephone rang. She happily answered, thinking Cliff was calling to say he was on his way for lunch, but a woman's voice shocked her out of her reverie. Katja could barely understand her. The lady had a heavy accent, one Katja had never heard. Eventually, she learned that the lady was Inez and was begging off to help Katja this day. One of her children was ill, and she did not wish to infect Katja or the children with the same bug. Was the patrona able to get by without her help? Yes, Katja assured the woman, and thanked her for her thoughtfulness

Chapter Seven

She had barely hung up the phone when another bell sounded. Katja was perplexed and the children a bit frightened. They all looked at each other with alarm. What was that? Maybe that was the big clock in the front hall? Katja surmised, but instantly her mind rejected that idea. She had not heard that chime all morning. There it sounded again, twice in a row. Sasha came into the kitchen, to search for the sound. He walked towards the front of the house. A dark shadow was obscuring the light coming in the window of the front door.

"Mama, there is someone at the front door." Katja came and opened the door up just a slit. A man in an ill-fitting brown uniform was standing in front of the door. It frightened her momentarily until she remembered where she was.

184

"Ikaeteina Novovovoskei?"

"Da, Ekatarina Novorotskaya is me."

"I got a box here for you. It's way too heavy for what we normally deliver." He scolded.

"Yes, is right, I sent big box from Russia. Is mine."

"Where do you want it?" He bent down to pick the box up again.

"Oh, here, is good. Thank you. Is there bill?"

"No, you paid for it, when you shipped it."

The man put the box down in the entrance hall, as Katja indicated and then was off again in a rush.

But Katja was happy. She called to the children, "Our box has come, our box is here!"

The children took up the cry, "The box is here; our box is here!" They all danced around the container. Irina wanted to open it right away. Katja had another idea.

"Let's wait 'till your Papi has time to look at everything with us. Won't that be a surprise for him?"

"When is my Papi coming?"

"In just a little bit. He'll be here soon."

Katja left the big carton in the middle of the entry way. She knew how heavy that box was. She had mailed it after all and had to struggle with it to get it downstairs from her attic rooms to where Oleg could put it in his sleigh, and then deliver it to the little office from where it was shipped out. Oleg, had helped her, letting her add her shipment to another he had going to that place.

The soup was just about ready, Katja tested the meat and potatoes and found them done. She turned down the heat under the pot to barely on, to keep everything warm, but not to cook it anymore. She put out bowls and spoons, bread, butter and knives.

Katja thought she might as well see what she could do about the laundry. She played with the knobs of the washing machine, and found that by twisting them she achieved different water temperatures. She figured that the numbers meant a certain amount of washing time. So, she turned the knob on the machine for the hottest water and the longest time and added whites to the machine. Then she added soap. She figured that the cap on the liquid soap bottle indicated the amount for a normal wash and just for good measure added a little more of the liquid soap.

The phone rang again, just as she was pretty happy with the results of her excursion into the utility room. Cliff told her he would be home in just a few minutes. Was there anything she needed?

"No, just come home. Lunch is ready." Quickly, she added some kielbasa sausage to the pot and turned the heat under her soup up just a bit.

It was not long before there was a noise in the garage, and the door opened. Cliff was home. As he entered the house, he called out:

"Hi, I'm home. Mmm, something sure smells good."

"Papi, Papi, Mama made my favorite soup and there is lots of meat in it," and switching the subject, Irina informed him, "Our box came, Papi. A man in uniform brought it, but he sure was grumpy."

"And which box might that be?" Cliff was thinking that some of the purchases they had shipped from Dallas had arrived.

"The one Mama mailed from home with all our special things in it. Can we open it now?"

"Irina, we are going to eat first, and then, if your Papi is able to stay home, we will open the box. Besides, you have to take your nap after lunch."

"But Mama, I'm not at all tired." she countered.

"It does not matter; nap time is nap time, and you two will have to lay down for at least an hour. You know that. There is no discussion on the matter."

"We did not have to take a nap at the hotel or on the train. We're big now Mama."

"Not that big yet. And we're home now. The old rules apply. Go wash your hands you two." Katja put a strict face on, and the children complied.

They ate, Cliff having seconds and commenting how wonderful it was to be able to come home to a hot meal. They chatted a bit. She asking how his day was going, and he wanted to know how she got along in the kitchen. She blushed.

"Everything good. I open doors to shelves to find where things go. Easy! Same with cooking. Open all doors, find what I need. Have problem with light." She blushed more, being quite nervous.

"Think I broke very much. Turn on all lights in kitchen to learn what switch turn on what light. One make terrible noise. No light come on. I so sorry."

He laughed. "No, you did not break anything. Here let me show you." They both got up and went into the kitchen.

"Is this the noise?"

"Da."

"It's the garbage disposal. See here, let me show you." With that, he stuffed the vegetable residue into the sink, turned on the water, and let the machine perform its task.

"See, you broke nothing. The garbage disposal just makes a lot of noise." He smiled at Katja.

"So, what's in that big box anyhow. Aren't you going to open it?"

"I'd like you to be here when we open it. Can you stay for a little while?"

"Sure. The snow is melting. By this evening, things will be back to normal. The animals can forage for themselves for a while."

"But first, Rina and Sasha have to take their naps. It was a long day yesterday and I can see that they are still tired."

"Mama, I'm not sleepy. I slept so much last night." Irina was wheedling.

"No, you have to have a nap." The little girl was upset, and Katja told her that her temper was an indication of how tired she really was.

"But Mama, I really don't have to take a nap. I'm big now. And I did not take a nap at home all the time anymore."

"You do not have to sleep, Sasha, but you, too, have to rest a while. Close your eyes to rest them, too. You may get up after thirty minutes, if you're not asleep." Both children went grudgingly toward their bedrooms.

"Papi, come please. We have to show you first all our things from home." Irina grabbed Cliff's hand and pulled him towards her room. He went willingly. Wondering what Katja had brought that the children thought to be so special.

There on a shelf in Irina's room were a pair of white toe shoes. Another shelf held an old doll in Russian clothing. The doll had a porcelain face and hands and what seemed to be real human hair. On another shelf were Russian stacking dolls, the prettiest he had ever seen. Finally, there was doll house furniture. It was handmade and painted. It was most beautifully painted. It resembled what he had always thought a Russian farmer's cottage was like on the inside. Katja was explaining.

"The ballet slippers were my grandmother's. The doll probably belonged to my grandfather's sister. Papa said he had found the toys in the dacha when he returned to it in 1918. There were no girls in his family, just his brother and him. There had been

190

girls in the earlier generations. He did not think that the doll was much older than the mid 1830's. His aunt was a little girl then, and her father had been on a mission to France in 1832. The doll house furniture is much older than that, though. He thought that whatever children had gone to the dacha had brought toys along to keep themselves entertained and then left them behind for future use."

"Children played with these toys? They had to have been very careful. All these things look new, even the toe shoes."

"Grandmother wore the shoes when she danced as Prima Ballerina and Grandfather saw her for the first time. They are worn, but she kept them always. How they wound up at the dacha is a mystery. Papa never told me. Perhaps he brought them himself, when he returned to the dacha in 1918."

"Your grandmother was a ballerina? How interesting."

"Well, yes. She danced that one time as Prima Ballerina, when Grandfather saw her, and he immediately married her. He would never allow her to dance on stage after that, but she danced at home and at the palace, and she instructed the princesses on how to dance. It was her job after all."

"Where did your grandmother dance?"

"In St. Petersburg."

"No, I don't mean what town. What company?"

"The Imperial Ballet."

"You're kidding, right? Your grandma danced for the Czar and his family?"

"Yes. She was an aristocrat in her own right, being the only child of a baron with a hereditary title. When she was young, she wanted to dance, and so she joined the ballet at about seven years of age. The dance mistress thought she was too old, but she managed to catch up. By the time she was fourteen years old, she regularly danced with the troop, but she danced only that one time as the Prima Ballerina, when she was about eighteen years old. Living in St. Petersburg, it was not so hard for her to get in. Papa said the company needed the good will of some of the nobles in order to have enough sponsors. So, Grandmama was in."

"You astound me even more. Your grandmother was a baroness?"

"Yes. My uncle would have inherited the title, but Papa found some papers where his mother made him her heir. I have the papers and the will. Still, by custom, Uncle Ivan should have inherited the title. Papa never found out what happened to him. He was, after all, in St. Petersburg that fall and winter of 1917/18.

"Mr. Papi, you must see my treasures, too." Aleksandr was pulling Cliff towards his room. "I have some special things too."

"Sure, let's see what you have!" Cliff could not imagine what the boy might have that was so important, but there on the shelf was a barnyard with all the animals that could be found on old McDonald's farm: horses and cattle and pigs and hens and a magnificent rooster, some ducks and geese. Upon further inspection, he found several breeds of horses were represented, huge, heavy limbed draft horses and splendid carriage horses, even racing Arabians. The cattle, too, represented several lineages. So did the sheep and goats. Cliff could have gotten down with the boy in an instant and played with him. Then, there were the toy soldiers. There must have been a whole regiment, complete with mounted officers, foot soldiers, flag carriers and buglers. There was heavy armament with attending men.

"My God, those are beautiful. I've never seen a set so complete."

"Papa said that it was once a whole army, but many of the soldiers have been melted down for lead balls during the war, when Napoleon invaded the country."

"These toys are older than the Napoleonic wars? They belong in a museum. They are beautiful, and the farm too. I've seen barnyards before, but nothing like this. I'm speechless."

"Do you like them, Mr. Papi?"

"Sasha, they are wonderful. You have to be very careful with them, not to damage the beautiful paint on all these figures. You are a very lucky boy to have such a beautiful set of toys."

"Will you play with me sometimes, please?"

"Yes, I'd love to."

"My father told me that the boys in the family learned strategies with these toys early in life, so, when they had to go to war, they knew how to place their men and win the battle."

"The men in your family were officers?"

"Da, certainly." Cliff's head was spinning. Katja certainly was not the peasant he had imagined. What other surprises did she have in store for him?

"The children need to take their nap, Mr. Cliff. Come, let's unpack the box." Cliff followed her back to the family room. The thoughts in his mind were bewildering. He could not comprehend all that she was telling him.

"If your father inherited that title, then you are a baroness now? Right?"

"So many ifs. And there are no more titles in Russia since the Bolsheviks took over and the Communists abolished all rank. Come, let's see if everything is in the box." She pulled him toward the hall.

"Why would something not be there? Does the carton look like someone opened it? Why would anyone tamper with the mail?"

"So many family things, important things. They knew how to open boxes without leaving a sign, they did. Communist take what they like. You have knife? You help me, yes?" Cliff produced his pocket knife and carefully slid the packing tape open. Gingerly Katja lifted a few items wrapped in linen away.

"Is everything there? Has anything been disturbed?"

Slowly, a big happy smile spread over Katja's face. "I think is okay." She unwrapped a long thin saber with a beautiful guard of gold and silver. She held it up.

"You like?"

"My God, where did you get that? It's

beautiful and worth a fortune."

"Is Grandfather's, and great Grandfather's and Grandfather before him. Is only ceremonial for when they go to palace to see Czar."

"Your grandfather saw the Czar?"

"Yes, he, how you say, advisor, councilor. See Czar many times, and also Czar before Nicolay. All family fathers see their Czar often."

"My god, Katja, who was your grandfather? Who is your family?"

"Grandfather was Count Petr Petrovitch Novorotsky. All oldest sons in family Count Novorotsky. All go to palace often. Must serve their Czar in some way. Is in books I have. Wait I will show you. You can read yourself, but first we unpack this." Cliff was dumbstruck. He could not imagine Katja's family being at court. Yet it seemed they had been. She took it all so for granted.

She is a Duchess also, if her uncle did not survive. Cliff thought, but did not mention that just now. He knew, she could not admit that, even to herself.

Next, she removed a small wooden box, beautifully finished and painted with some sort of emblem. She opened it. The box contained two beautiful identical pistols, ivory handles and engraved and inlaid with gold and silver, dueling pistols.

"Anybody ever use these?"

"No, I do not think so. They were a gift to my ancestor from his Czar. Here are two old rifles, too. They were used, I think. I had friend take apart. Can you put back together?"

"I hope so. If not, I'll take them to a friend, who is a gunsmith. These two are beautiful. We will have to have them insured and put away into our gun safe. I would not trust having these laying around."

She had produced the barrels out of a magnificent samovar. Where she had hidden them, wrapped in fine leather. She produced three more smallish magnificent boxes from the inside of the tea maker. Carefully, Katja opened the first box. Inside wrapped in silk and velvet nestled a magnificent jewel-encrusted egg. Just one look convinced him that he was looking at one of the fabled Faberge eggs

"Czar Nicolay gave this to my grandparents as a wedding present. There are two more. One he gave Grandfather for his services one year, when he spent most of the year at court advising the Czar, and the other one was given to Grandmother for all her work with the princesses, and staying with them for an entire year, and not going to Grandfathers estate with him."

"Katja, do you have any idea of the value of these trinkets? You could have sold them and never had to worry about money again."

"No, could not sell. People do not buy such things when they are hungry. Everyone in my village is hungry. Also, it was much too dangerous to sell these when the Communists were in charge. It would have identified Papa as a noble, and all nobles were imprisoned and eventually killed. Only in the West are these things valuable. Papa told me these items are important family heirlooms and to never give them up." It occurred to Cliff instantly, that not only was Katja's father a noble, but so was she and the children. It seemed to have no effect on Katja. He was quite sure, that she had never thought that she might be special.

"I guess, he was right in that. We have to have them appraised and insured and put them in a safe place. They should go to Sasha and Irina. I have never seen one of these eggs before, but they are famous. Everyone knows about them and how valuable they are. There were not very many made, and most have been accounted for. That you should have three is incomprehensible. What other treasures have you in that box?"

Katja removed another container from the box. This one seemed quite heavy. She handled it gingerly. Again, it was a beautiful container, wrapped in some more linen to protect the box. The lid of which sported again a Crest or Coat of Arms of some sort. Inside was a set of china in the typical Russian pattern of blue and gold on a white back ground. Only these had in the middle again that same, colorful, crest. It was a small lunch set or tea service for four consisting of cups, saucers and dessert plates, as well as one larger platter, one small tea pot, sugar and creamer containers.

"Is that your family's coat of arms?"

"What is coat of arms?"

"A family crest or sign identifying the family."

"Da, is same on everything and on Grandfather's ring to seal letter with."

"You have that seal, also?"

"Da, I have all the things needed to prove family is Count Novorotsky. But is not good anymore. No more Counts, no more Barons, no more Czars. Is just what is important to family. To show children what we once were, and if history had turned out differently, we still might be. Papa always told me to keep these things and upon my death, they are to go to my son, so that if the law ever changes again, our family should rise again, and have the items required to prove our status. It is just something to instill pride in family in our children and perhaps, urge them to greater effort throughout their lives."

Katja rummaged again in the packing box. This time she produced a black lacquer box emblazoned with a flowery design and another, different coat of arms. This new container was beautiful, although not very big, about the size of the jewelry box Cliff had once given his wife as a Christmas present. It even had two drawers in the bottom half. Katja's smile was dreamy, happy. She opened the lid and lifted out a small tiara, made entirely of a clear sparkling stone. Then she pulled out the little drawers. Several clear colored glass baubles were nestled in their silk slots. She started to select some and fitted them into the little tiara.

"Why all the fuss about these rhinestones? Your family sure put trinkets into a most impressive receptacle."

"What is rhinestones, please?"

"Imitation gems, for costume jewelry. Nice, but not so expensive. Glass baubles."

"Is not glass baubles, Cliff. Is real jewels. Is Grandmama's tiara she had made from all her jewels to wear to court. Emblem is coat of arms of her family, the Barons Klymm. See, is different than Grandpapa's."

"Those are real? Oh, my God!" Cliff was

verging on a faint. His head was spinning. Katja was playing with the stones, showing him what a clever design the little tiara had. The stones could be exchanged at will, and so could also the necklace and earrings be enhanced to match any gown worn. Cliff was dry mouthed, hyper-ventilating.

"You packed that in just a big cardboard box. Oh my, I hope you had it insured."

"No, what is this insured? Mr. Cliff, are you all right? You don't look so good."

"Katja, we must insure all of it. It is just too valuable. To think you sent this uninsured is unimaginable."

"Cliff, darling, what is insure?"

"Insurance is to protect items, so that if they're lost or stolen, you get the money to replace them."

"Is of no value, is just important for family. No reason to get this insure. If people think something is important, they look and open and take. No, just a few family things, not important to someone else and cannot be replaced. Is one of a kind. Therefore, cannot be valued.

"I have just one more item here." She pulled a heavy wooden case out of the packing box. This container was obviously old. It had ornamental iron bands protecting the corners and along the middle embedded into the wood. The iron too seemed old. He had not seen such a design except in pictures showing early medieval artifacts. The criss-crossing iron belts were secured by a heavy iron lock. Katja produced a key from her chain and opened the box. She lifted the lid off. Inside was another container, this one of fine marquetry and embellished with gold. Carefully she removed the inside box and laid it on the table next to Cliff.

"The contents of this box are most important to family. They always go to oldest surviving son. If no son, maybe daughter, so maybe it's mine. Who can say if Uncle Ivan had family or if still alive. Anyway, is here now." With that, she opened the container, about the size of a boot box. It too was locked, and Katja selected another key on her chain and fitted it into the slot. The key was of a really old design. Presently, she lifted the lid. What she brought forth was stunning.

"This is crown of the count Novorotsky. Is made of gold, pearls, diamonds and amber. This is the seal that affirms orders of count. Is of great value to family. Grandfather was last count. He wore this crown a few times; when confirmed count, when presented to Czar, when marry Grandmama. Before him, all called Count Novorotsky wear same crown. When he set free serf, his signature of the order would be authenticated with this seal. When he presided over his court of law, he wear crown and validate verdict with this seal. Very important, you see."

"Yes, it is very important. I do not believe that any other Russian crown is in the west. Surely, there must be others. Maybe in the museums, like at the Kremlin or in St. Petersburg at the Hermitage."

"Papa did not think many survived, for the Bolsheviks destroyed everything that had to do with the, how you say, Czarist Regime? But, perhaps, some did survive. I do not know. I've never been to any of those places, safe for the few hours we spend in Moskva coming here."

"I realize, these beautiful items are important to you and your family. I think, however, they should be shared with the whole world and all the Russians. These items most certainly are National Treasures."

"No, I cannot give them up. Papa implored me never to part with them and to stress to the children that they are only important to our family. I should try to find out, if Uncle Ivan survived and had children. I should return these things to them then, but not anyone else." Katja was adamant.

Cliff looked at that treasure trove of heirlooms and did not know how to proceed. He only knew, he was not capable to properly preserve them. The shipping carton was finally empty, except for the wrapping that Katja had used to protect precious boxes. A closer look revealed that she had used exceptionally fine linen. The linen was embroidered and/or woven with the crest of the Novorotsky family.

All pieces were adorned with lace also. Cliff knew he was looking at more precious belongings of the family. He felt, that he was the guardian, protector of a heritage, that in his small rural home, he could not truly ensure the safety of these irreplaceable trappings of a lost culture. He did not know, how to contact someone who would be able to advise him on how to preserve these items for posterity, for they belonged to the Nation of Russia and to the children, an important legacy to be housed in vaults or a museum. Here, in his home, that legacy was vulnerable. He needed to protect all of it from theft, fire and natural disasters. He was sure no flood would damage all these beautiful objects. He felt they should be seen, but here, they were just too unprotected. Tornadoes were a frequent threat in the area. This was, after all, tornado alley.

He would have to caution Katja and the children never to mentions these heirlooms to any one, for if just one greedy person heard about this horde, these very precious belongings would be endangered. Yet, he also felt that these extraordinary pieces of family history should be on display in their home. The children must be steeped in and be comfortable with their birthright, their heritage. How could he ensure the safety of these precious heirlooms? He would have to ponder that problem.

Katja realized he was shocked by the impact and the importance of all these family heirlooms. She was unable to comprehend that they were truly extraordinary and of an importance far beyond her little family realm. She was almost afraid to show him the remainder of her treasures, still packed away in her suitcases.

Cliff suddenly remembered that the children had been absent during the unpacking of the box from Russia. He asked Katja if they should be awakened, but she assured him they would come tumbling out of their rooms the minute they woke.

"They are so beautiful when sleeping. Come, let us look." She picked up his hand as if pulling him away. Hand in hand, they tiptoed into first Irina's, and then Sasha's room. Both children were still sound asleep, Rina cuddling her Panda bear and Sasha hanging on to an older version. Leaving the room quietly, Cliff put his arm about Katja's shoulder. It was a natural gesture, one she responded to with encircling his waist with one of hers. He was delighted.

Cliff helped Katja find appropriate spaces for her family's heirlooms. The china and jeweled eggs, he had her display in the dining room china hutch, but the jewels and weapons, he requested she put into his gun safe for security until they could find a better place. She told him there were more, still packed away in her suitcases. They were interrupted, though, before they ever got a chance to unpack those items.

Chapter Eight

The doorbell rang, and when Cliff answered, all this friends stood on the porch with a banner, flowers galore and covered dishes. The banner read "Welcome Home, Katja."

Everyone rushed into the house at once. The women all tried at once to kiss her and the men tried to pump her hand. One or two also hugged her, and all welcomed her and the children to Oklahoma, the States, Cimarron County and the town of Boise City. They all invited her to their homes. There were, of course, Don and Donna Brewer, the Garzas with their two grandchildren and youngest daughter, the other county commissioner with his family. There were the District Attorney with his wife and little daughter, Cliff's banker and wife, as well as his accountant

Noah Wyllie and wife Carrol. Doctor Eli Magnussen and his son and daughter and Jack Riley the local pharmacist also showed up. The mayor of Boise city brought his family, and a couple of the neighboring ranchers came with their wives and children. Suddenly, the house was full to bursting.

Inez and Donna took over the food and arranged it buffet style on the bar to the kitchen. Another woman took care of all the plants. They all had brought either Amaryllises or Poinsettias in the most gorgeous shades of red. Instantly, the house looked festive. Sasha and Irina came out of their rooms still sleepy, when they heard all the commotion. The sight of children wiped away any thoughts of more rest.

Soon, the children were running all in and out of the house, playing catch, hide and seek and blind man's bluff. Katja was amazed at how well all the children got along. It was so good to see her own two running and laughing with the others. She could not remember such boisterous play ever in Russia. It was much too cold to play outside for such a large part of the year, and people lived in such cramped quarters that only quiet play could be tolerated inside. When dusk fell, Inez and Donna had completed dinner preparations. All the children were seated and served in the breakfast area and at the kitchen bar. The adults filled plates and cups and found spaces wherever they could.

Katja had never experienced such a party. She felt a little taken aback that the women should take over her kitchen, but she had to admit that this was nice and very thoughtful of Mr. Collins' friends. She could also not imagine why she felt so proprietary about the kitchen. She was not even familiar yet with this kitchen, and these women obviously were. Once she figured out that Inez was the same woman as the lady who was to help her with the house and that Donna was the Donna, who was married to the Sherriff Don, and therefore truly one of Mr. Cliff's oldest friends, she was able to banish the slight irritation.

Everyone was vying for her attention. She quickly realized everyone was as curious about life in Russia as she was about life in America. The women all asked every conceivable question about the lot of women in Russia. How was it different than in America? Did she like it here? She tried to answer all. Often, though, her language skills failed her. She finally asked Cliff about the curiosity about her country.

"Doesn't the news report what is going on in Russia? I thought your press reports everything."

"Yes, it does," she was told, "but your government does not allow our press free access to your country. Even if a reporter is admitted, what he can report is censored, sometimes even confiscated, so we have very few reliable reports about living conditions in your country. We hear stories, but they are so bad that we do not believe them. We just figure it is in our government's interest to distribute bad propaganda about your land."

After that, she tried to answer the questions honestly and to the best of her ability. Many questions, she did not comprehend. Others, she was unable to answer because she had not been in the US long enough for a comparison or to make judgments. But she gave frank and candid answers, whenever possible.

Most people left about 8:00 P.M. Only a few true old friends stayed longer. Donna and Inez cleaned up before they left, but at the end there, the three couples sat around the coffee table in the living area, engrossed in deep conversation. Even the children were allowed to participate. Their observances were poignant and direct and helped everyone understand the immigrants just a little better. By 10:00 P.M., even these last visitors left. On the way out to their car, Donna whispered to Cliff that he had chosen the right one, she felt, and to her husband, she said she thought Cliffy would be very happy.

Three days later, Katja finally found time for a long letter to her friends in Russia. She had a tough time putting everything down on paper and had to start over a couple of times.

My dearest friends!

We have finally arrived in our new home. All is well. Mr. Collins is such a nice man and so handsome. He is almost bald, but that does not detract from his appeal. He is over two meters tall and has very blue eyes. His hair seems to be dark blond, what there is left of it. And he is smooth shaven at all times. When he is not working outside, he uses a pleasing cologne. Most of the time his head is covered by a silver-gray cowboy hat. He also smiles a lot and is always cheerful. He is wonderful with the children. Even Sasha likes him. So much has happened in the last two weeks, it is hard to tell it all. Let me start at the beginning.

We arrived here late Sunday night in a snowstorm. Today is Friday. All the snow is gone. It is warm outside, above freezing. Can you imagine? But let me start at the beginning.

Our train to Yekaterinburg arrived four hours late. There was no time for dinner. We had only five minutes to change from one train to the other. We also had to change platforms. Tatiana, I must thank you again for the sandwiches. Our train was not equipped for a third meal and we shared our bounty with an old grandfather, who had entertained the children with folk tales all day. He is ill and under doctors' orders to eat at regular intervals. I was afraid he might get sick. Old Boris Mikhailovich helped me with adding the children's suitcases to the big cases, by strapping them together. In Yekaterinburg, he handed the children down to me and my luggage. Then we ran. The lady who served us tea all day, helped me to the other train. She was so very nice, but the conductor of that train is still living in the communist area. She was mean. The Trans-Siberian train took off before we had even reached our compartment.

You will not believe it. We met friends of Mr. Collins on this train. A family from England was in the next compartment. The children played the whole time, with Heather, the little daughter of the couple, teaching my children English. It was so very good to make friends, for we spend more than four days on that train. We arrived in Moscow just in time to go to bed and be ready to go to the airport at four the next morning. I had the driver of the taxi that had taken us to the hotel come back and she did!

In London, one of the Aeroflot stewardesses showed us the way to the American Airlines gate. I do not believe she is going back to Russia again. She introduced me to her husband, an English man. She thanked me for giving her the opportunity to slip away from the crew of our plane. We spend just a little less than an hour in England but never left the airport.

Once on the American plane, the surprises started. We had a row of seats next to the window, just behind first class, where there is a little more space to stretch out. The steward insisted that other passengers change seats with us. Then they brought *out toys for the children. They could actually sit on the floor and play. They also brought the children as many drinks as they wanted. Sasha fell in love with Coca Cola and Rina adores Orange Juice. Once we were in the air, the captain took the children to the cockpit. Sasha was very impressed.*

We arrived in Dallas in the middle of the afternoon, their time. It would have been midnight or later where you are. It took a very long time to get through the formalities at immigration. They did not search my luggage. We only had to answer some questions. They wanted to know if we brought food or vodka or fruits. How strange!

Mr. Collins was waiting for us in the reception area. He handed me the biggest bouquet of roses you can imagine. Roses in the middle of winter! The first flowers I have ever received from a man in my life. It was so hot in the airport. The children wanted to take their coats off. Just think, they wanted to run around in that big building without winter coats in December. Mr. Collins allowed it, even urged me to take mine off, too. I commented that the building was nicely heated. He told me the building was being cooled! That it would be warmer still outside. Now you know, I could not fathom that. But again, he was right. It was about twenty degrees Celsius outside, in December, just imagine!

Outside the building, cars were everywhere. Just like you can see on television. And in the parking garage, there were thousands of cars and trucks. Sasha asked if Mr. Collins has a car too? Yes, he does. Actually, he has two trucks, one is a passenger truck (they call it here a SUV, a sports utility vehicle) and the other is similar to what Walker, the ranger, drives on the television show.

Then he has several farm vehicles. But that we only learned yesterday. The passenger truck is unbelievably luxurious. It has leather seats and they have heating and cooling in them, not just in the vehicle. The seats actually get warm or cold, however you want it. There is a computer in that vehicle that tells you where you are, and how to get to your destination. You never get lost. There is a radio, CD player and a TV in it. You can watch movies while you are driving. He bought the children several of these CDs, so they would not get bored on the long way home.

Over the next few days, until Saturday, we did a lot of shopping. I got my hair cut and set and nails manicured. He bought me make up. We went to the zoo, and the aquarium, and an old-fashioned village.

We saw Christmas decorations, for the celebration of Christmas. It is a holiday similar to our old-time St. Nickolas day, or perhaps Epiphany. And we went shopping.

Always shopping for clothing for us. I now own six pair of shoes and the children each have three pair and house shoes. Sasha owns ten pair of jeans and even more shirts and sweaters. I lost count of what he bought for Irina. The child has matching tops and bottoms enough for one every day of the week, plus several dresses, and jeans and sweaters. We all got more coats and jackets. It is more than you can imagine. (That word shows up a lot in this letter, and it is also getting quite long.)

On the first day, here, he took us to the town of Fort Worth. It was only a few minutes' drive from our hotel in the town of Arlington. He showed Sasha were that Texas Ranger show is filmed.

It is the local hall of justice and one of the police officers showed us around on the inside. Sasha recognized quite of few places from the show. We had dinner in a very fine restaurant across the street from that big white hotel they sometimes show on that Ranger show. Sasha asked that you please tell Sergey of his adventures. We will also send pictures, as soon as we have them developed.

It is the little things that are most surprising. Like flowers blooming in December. There was no snow to be seen anywhere. I kept asking if there were palm trees in the Dallas area. Mr. Collins could not fathom my desire to see them. He said if I really wanted to see some, he would take me. They can be found in the towns of Austin or San Antonio or Houston and all along the coast. The nearest place is only a few hours' drive away. It was just all so

216

amazing.

There is a skating rink in a shopping center in the middle of Dallas. The shopping center is enormous, with hundreds of stores and restaurants. But in the middle of the bottom floor is an ice rink. The children can skate there even though the temperature in the building is about 18 degrees Celsius. People walk around in shorts, and go skating!

The roads in this Texas State are also very unique. The major intersections have multiple lanes crossing above and below one other. The bridges are so high, you think you will wind up in the sky. They scare both Mr. Collins and me, but the children love them. There are no such interchanges in our little town. I am thankful for that, for Mr. Collins told me, I will have to learn to drive the big SUV truck. I am to take Sasha to school and pick him up daily and I must learn, so I can go shopping.

Shopping is a most important thing in America. You go shopping for food or clothing or shoes, or furniture or towels. One does not pick up the evening meal on one's way home from work from a government owned meal preparation station.

Mr. Collins bought enough food for us all for a whole month. I am to cook every meal. You can imagine how happy that makes me. I will not have to save kopeks enough for one meal. I won't have to search in my trousers for the last coin to obtain a cup of soup and a crust of bread. I can bake my own. I have a bread machine and all I have to do, is pour in the flour and yeast and turn the thing on. If I want to bake a cake I can choose from several packages in the pantry and just add eggs and milk and mix it up and put the batter in a pan in the electric oven and in no time, do I have a cake. And there are gallons of ice-cream in the freezer to go with the cake. We have freezers and refrigerators to store all that food. Amazing!

Why I worry so, that I made the right choice, I do not know. Should I have chosen another man? No, I am sure this man is a good husband for me. I do not know how Irina could tell from the picture this is a very nice man. I do not know how she was so sure, but I am glad I listened to her. Mister Collins is a very nice, handsome, caring and thoughtful man. I could never have found anyone better.

I did get a big scare yesterday, twice. The first time was when I turned on lights in the kitchen. Mister Collins said Inez is coming to help me with the house work and I say it is very fine. The children and I will be alone for little while, to learn our new home. So, as I said, I turned on all lights in the kitchen to find where everything is. Only when I turned one switch, there is a terrible noise. Scary! I turned it off quick. I am so scared that I damaged Mr. Collins beautiful house.

Mr. Collins is not mad at all. I did not break anything. It just makes lots of noise. Mr. Collins is perplexed that I not know about this peelings eater. Now, I am confused. He showed me. You put all soft food trash in the sink, turn the water on and the switch, and machine in the sink eats up all food residue. Such a thing has never been. He assured me all kitchens have a sink with an eating machine.

The second time I got very scared is when someone rings a bell. I do not know where the sound comes from. We search. Sasha sees a man standing outside the door through the glass window in the door. I go to see what he wants. It is man in uniform. Like a soldier. I am so scared. Maybe they want to take us back to Russia. But he had my box. Everything is good. All my things are there and we do not have to go back to Russia. I am so happy.

Mr. Collins promises me that we will marry soon, so that I am not scared anymore. He wanted to wait to make sure I am happy with him. Until I am sure I want him, but   I am so very sure now. He is a good, loving, kind husband. I will marry him soon.

There are so many more things to tell you. They will have to await another day. Mr. Collins will be here shortly. He wants to introduce me to the bank manager, so I will be able to withdraw funds for shopping, and so I may write checks.

I should say in closing that we are all well.

The children love this house, their rooms and the new man in our lives. I should also assure you that Mister Collins exaggerated nothing in his letters. I would say he was quite reticent and not boastful. I wish I could share my good fortune with all of you.

I wish to tell Olga, she need not worry about her little bird. Irina is happier than I've seen her ever. She loves the big white cat Mr. Collins allows her to sleep with. The animal is beautiful and very gentle. She seems to enjoy Rina as much as the child likes her. And can you believe it, Aleksandr has made friends with a huge white dog? Snowball belongs to Mr. Collins and is a working dog, but you would be surprised where the animal sleeps, da, right with Sasha.

Tatiana, please be so kind and let Oleg and Olga read this letter, and also, tell Sergey and his mother how well we are. I shall write soon again. Although I am so very happy, I miss all of you. I shall forever treasure the good times we had.

Until very soon

Katja.

Chapter Nine

The next few days flew by in a flurry. Packages arrived steadily with the items they had purchased in Dallas. On nice days, the children played outside with their new toys or just explored the ranch. The Garza children and grandchildren came over to play. Sasha went with Cliff to inspect the horses and cattle. He loved going with Mr. Cliff. Irina was busy around the house with dolls and the cat. In the late afternoon and early morning, the children watched television to help them with their English. Even Katja benefitted from the shows by learning more English.

Soon, they were clamoring for a Christmas tree like at their friend's home, and so on Friday afternoon, Cliff bundled up the family in the big SUV, and they went to town to obtain a pretty spruce. Of course, the children wanted the tallest tree available. Cliff could not convince them that it would not fit into the house. They finally settled on a nine-foot blue spruce. Of course, the children were clamoring to put the tree up immediately. Katja was dismayed at her offspring's unacceptable behavior. What was Mr. Cliff thinking? She would have to chastise them in private severely.

Mr. Cliff, however, was grinning from ear to ear. Finally, the kids were behaving with some spontaneity and not like scarred little urchins. He confided in Katja that he was as impatient as the children to see the tree decorated. It had been such a long time since he had a tree in his house, and never in this new house.

So, maybe, if it was all right with her, they could pick up pizza on the way home for supper and then get started on that beautiful tree. Of course, the word "pizza" did not escape two sets of listening ears, and the meaning was remembered and the children instantly begged for the treat. Again, Katja was appalled by her children's behavior. What was happening to them? She could not recall such begging and clamoring as they were displaying. Mr. Cliff must think she had not taught them anything and that he had invited unruly and demanding Mongols to his home.

Cliff was not thinking any such thing. Finally, the kids were secure enough with him to act like children are wont to do. After only a few days with them, he was loving them. Rina had made that easy from the beginning by her unreserved acceptance of him, and calling him Papi had been more than he could have asked for. Sasha too was a fine child. He was so serious and responsible and willing to help all the time, just like a little adult. Finally, he was being a boy, asking for things, even clamoring for a treat. Yeah, he could love that little guy with all his heart. He knew, too, that they had never had Christmas before, and he was enjoying them enjoying the holiday, before it was too late and the inevitable knowledge should take some of the wonder of the day away. He smiled happily, and Katja saw it and wondered what he was thinking about.

On their way home, they stopped by Walmart and picked up a goodly supply of tree decorations. He knew they did not have nearly enough lights and tinsel and garlands at home. Katja was appalled at the expenditures once again, and when Irina found another box of silver balls, Katja had her put it firmly back. Cliff only smiled and put it back in the cart.

"You are spoiling them so very much. Is not good for them, Mr. Cliff," she admonished.

"Katja, Christmas comes only once a year, and children need to enjoy it. We will save all this stuff for next year, and then they will be cherished memories for the children. This year is the year they will truly enjoy Christmas, before they are grown up too much, and the magic is tarnished. Christmas is the reason why I had to hurry you so to come over here, so the children should have the experience, so please let me indulge them. They are such well-behaved little ones. I love participating in their enjoyment. Besides, every parent wants to make the holiday as special as possible for their children. That is what it's all about."

He smiled at her, and she could see that he really had as much fun as the children did, and she nodded with tears once again in her eyes. *How have I ever gotten so lucky to have this truly wonderful man come into my life*, she thought.

Cliff saw the tears, "I'm sorry, Sweetie. I did not want to upset you. If you really think I'm doing too much, then we won't, but think about it, please."

"I not upset Mr. Cliff, I so very happy. Can't believe I so lucky to have found you. Thank you."

"Naw, you don't have to thank me, Sweetie. Let's just enjoy the season. Besides I'm the lucky one." Then he gave her a big hug and smooch in the store, and to heck with whoever might see how happy he is.

Once home, he mounted the tree in the new tree stand while Katja and the children put dinner on the table. After they had finished eating and the dishes were stacked in the dish washer, Cliff asked the children in a very serious voice.

"Now then, where shall we place the tree? Anyone have any ideas?"

"Right here in the middle of the room." That was Aleksandr's suggestion.

"No, we can't do that, you dummy. We won't be able to watch *telebision*." Rina countered.

"Where then? There is furniture everywhere."

"Should we put it in the front hall. There is no furniture there?" Cliff asked, semi-serious.

The children were deep in thought. Rina brightened, "We could put it on the mantle."

"No, Rina, it's too big for that," her brother countered.

"Maybe we can move the TV into our bedroom, and we can put the tree in its spot." Cliff suggested. The children thought about that but did not quite like that idea. They had learned to like watching TV in the mornings and more on cold days.

"Papi, maybe we could move some other furniture to make space for our big tree. Would that be okay?" Rina was asking.

"I think that is a great idea, Irina. So, where would you like to put it, in front of the windows? Or over there next to the back door or maybe next to the fireplace, or we could put it in the library or in the dining room?" Everyone thought about those ideas.

Irina thought it would be nice next to the fireplace, like you see on TV. It would also be nice in one of the front windows, so people who came to the house could see it from outside.

Katja suggested they put it in front of the big windows in the living area. That way, anyone who came to visit could see the tree as soon as they entered the house, and it was visible to all in the house. She might enjoy looking at it while cooking their dinner, and even while the kids were eating their lunch or breakfast, they could admire their tree. They would only have to move one chair and a little table out of the way, and that could be easily accomplished. Cliff asked Sasha to help him with the furniture, and Irina was to move the smaller things and to tell the men where she wanted everything. He'd winked at their mother and whispered to her.

"This way, they will feel important. I'll place the chairs so it will look okay."

Finally, it was time to bring the tree in and place it in its assigned spot. With much ado, the tree was finally turned in such a way to insure its best view to the room. Then they started to decorate. Cliff held Irina in his arms while she placed the angel at the very top. Next, Cliff and Aleksandr strung tiny electric lights all along the branches, making sure the wires were hidden well. Once all the lights had been attached, the honor fell to Katja to plug in the lights. Oh, how beautiful their tree already was, even without all the other decorations.

Slowly, cautiously, all the glass balls found their way to just the right spots. Everyone participated. Katja was assigned to watch out that no area of the green tree remained empty of decoration. When all the boxes had been emptied, Cliff finished off the tree by putting on the tinsel. All the lights were doused in the room. Only the lights on the tree remained on, and everyone was breathless by the wonder of the glittering Christmas tree. Katja had to get the camera, so they could take pictures of the first Christmas tree the children had ever known, and to send pictures of the marvel back to their friends in Russia.

It was long after the children's normal bedtime that the tree was finally completed. All the excitement had tuckered little Irina out. She was sitting in her favorite chair, thumb in mouth, sound asleep. When Aleksandr attempted to wake her, Cliff stopped him. He took one final picture of the little girl and then gently picked her up and carried her to her bed.

Two days later, Cliff brought all their developed film home. He had sacks of pictures, for there had been copious pictures taken while in Dallas and now even more and all the film Katja had shot in Russia. He took the afternoon off, and together the family walked him through the little village of Novorotskoye in the Ural Mountains of Russia. He now saw the pictures of the people Katja and the children had talked about so much. He finally had an idea of the cramped quarters in which they had lived, and of the hardships involved in just bringing up a load of coal or going to the bathroom and having to stand in line waiting for the facility to become vacant. The dacha, he felt, was large, a nice country cottage for a large, active family, now the home for several families. He could not imagine the tiny living space they all had, but now he could understand his family's wonderment at all the space they had in their new home.

Chapter Ten

The following morning Sasha asked: "Will you please write a letter to Sergey for me? Mama, I will help you with your chores. If we don't write him soon, I am afraid he will forget me." And so, after making beds and starting the dishwasher and a load of wash, Katja brought out a writing tablet and pen. Her son dictated a letter to his best friend who he missed dreadfully.

Sergey;

I wish I could talk to you to tell you all that has happened to us since we left the dacha. I thought, I would be able to write this letter, but I still have not learned to write. Mama is writing down what I tell her.

There are so many things to tell you about that

I don't know where to start. I am afraid I will forget something important. Like forgetting how to speak Russian. I already forgot some words because we have to speak English here. I found out about that from our friend Heather who we met on the train to Moscow. She told us only Russians speak Russian and most people speak English. Only Jorge and his family speak Spanish and I have a hard time understanding them sometimes. David and his sister live with his grandparents. Inez helps Mama in the house here and Jorge, the grandfather, works for Mister Cliff.

Please tell Oleg Mikhailovich not to worry about us. Mr. Cliff is very nice to us. He has never hit any of us, not even Mama when she almost broke his house. He just laughed and showed her what to do and gave her a big hug and a kiss. I have never seen him drink vodka. He does not get mean. He sometimes drinks a little wine with mama, and on very special occasions they have something they call champagne. But he is never drunk or mean. Tell Oleg that, for I know he worries.

It took ever so long to get to Moscow. The trains were so slow in arriving everywhere. It was a good thing we made friends on the trains. Heather taught us English and it is a good thing too, for it helped me understand Mr. Cliff.

Things got better right away once we got to the West. In London, the stewardess helped us find our plane to Texas. She was Russian, but I don't think she is going back ever again. She introduced us to her English husband and he was thanking Mama for giving his wife an excuse to get away from the other Russians. Then on that new big plane, we got super good seats, and the pilot came and took me to the cockpit, and showed me how he flies the plane. You should have seen it, Sergey, I never know, how he knew what all the dials and switches were for. It was so cool.

And then the new stewardesses brought us whatever we wanted to drink. I got Coca Colas, you should taste them, they are so good and Irina got orange juice. She thinks that is the best stuff ever and we got two meals on that plane. The food tasted really good.

I think I fell asleep for a while because it took no time at all and we were in Texas and it was warm there. The sun was shining and it was so warm we took off our coats and hats and mittens. There was not even any snow on the ground and they had flowers on the sidewalks. Mama says she is going to send our warm coats to you and Elena, because we don't need them anymore, besides we have grown so much, they don't fit us anymore.

Please tell Olga Kerchenova not to worry about her little bird. Mr. Collins just gives her everything she ever wants. I don't think our real Papa would have adored her as he does.

On our first day here in America, he took us to see the Hall of Justice where Walker Texas Ranger was made. The police man even showed us the office he had. It is all real, not make belief. I saw many places for real that are in that show. It really is all there. And it is here on TV also, I watch it every day. Only here they speak English, and not Russian like at home. Mama says here is home now, the dacha no longer is. I guess she is right about that.

We spent a lot of days in Texas doing fun stuff. We went to two zoos and to an amusement park they had lit up for Christmas. It was a real fairy land. I liked a lot of the animals at the zoo. Mr. Cliff told us we would come back in the spring, when all of the animals are outside. Now, he thought, a lot of them are sleeping, because it is too cold. But it was not cold at all. We were even wearing summer clothes. Then he took us to an old-time village. He said it is similar to how the people lived in Texas and Oklahoma over a hundred years ago. Sergey, it looked a lot like Novorotskoye only much smaller.

We went ice skating once inside this big building. There were a lot of stores in this building, where we bought clothes and Mama got her hair done and we bought toys and books and in the middle of that building was the ice rink. We skated in shorts. It was so unbelievable. Mr. Cliff bought us all clothes and toys for Irina and me. I have now jeans for every day of the week and then some and I have three pairs of shoes and house slippers. I would love to share

233

them with you. Mama is going to send you our new heavy winter coats. The ones Mr. Cliff sent to us in Russia. We don't need them anymore. It does not get so cold here and there is seldom snow, besides the coats are too small. We have already grown so much.

It would be so much fun to have you here to play with. We could share my new big room and all the toys that we now have. Of course, our dog would like you like he likes me, and Elena could cuddle the cat so she might have a rest from our Irina. You would love my room. I have a big star on the wall, like the star Walker wears on his shirt, only much bigger, and the cover on my bed is made like jeans and it has a cowboy on it swinging a lasso. My bed is big enough for both of us to sleep in comfortably.

I have a desk in my room, and a rocking chair, where I can sit and read all my new books. Yes, I am learning to read. And there is plenty of space on the floor for us to stretch out and play games. My room is larger than our living room in the dacha. Irina's room is just as big. And we don't need wardrobes, because they are built into the room and much bigger than our one wardrobe at the dacha. And we never have to hide under the bed, Mr. Cliff just never gets mean, like Ilya.

Sergey, I miss you so much. Mr. Cliff promised that I would see you again, only he does not know when, only that it will be a long time from now. Please do not forget me.

Your friend forever

Sasha

Chapter Eleven

Once Katja had finished writing the letter to her son's friend, she was thinking about how she came to be writing that letter. Could it be that she had been in America less than four weeks? Could it be that it was only a little more than three months that she had even heard of that wonderful man she was about to marry in a few more days? It had all happened so quickly. Oh, but how wonderful it was, that she had taken that chance and followed her daughter's instinct and came to be with Mr. Collins. In less than two weeks, she would be his wife. To be honest, she could hardly wait.

Was she being unfaithful to her deceased husband Sergey? Yes, she had loved him, and he had loved her, but for Mr. Collins, her feelings were much

236

different. There was excitement for him and she could hardly wait for him to come home, for him to kiss her, for the two of them to be alone in their room. This kind of urgency had never entered her being with Sergey. They had married because it was convenient; it was expected; it made life easier. They had lived their own lives side by side.

Here, with Mr. Collins, they both shared each other's lives. He took delight in her accomplishments and complimented her on her looks, the food she prepared, even the way she raised her children. Sergey had expected all of that but never complimented her about anything. All of her good fortune had come about because she and Tatiana had sent their stories and pictures to that magazine on a lark. That had been on a day when they both were so downtrodden, depressed and worried about how to survive for another week, another month, another year in the drudgery to which they both had been condemned by the circumstances of their birth.

And then the first letter had arrived, and then the second, and with it, that box and her and her children's lives had been changed forever. She could remember those letters by heart. She would always remember those eventful days when they arrived in her home and in her heart, and while her children sat and watched television and dreamt of Christmas presents, Katja remembered those letters and days.

She had taken his letter to her best friend,

Tatiana Bukhachev, to help her with understanding all that it contained. Tatiana had been better in English in school than she, and she hoped her friend might also know someone to give her English lessons.

The tone of the letter was not boastful; still both women thought it was, for they could not comprehend that a bachelor would have a house of that size. Yet, Katja remembered her father telling her that the entire dacha had once been used by his family, and that at most for a month during hunting season and that not even every year. She also remembered him saying that the villa in St. Petersburg had enough room for lavish entertaining and bedrooms for every member of the family and guest suites for several visitors. The estate residence was huge with individual apartments for the more important members of the family and their intimate servants, as well as public rooms and more family rooms assigned to different functions and the servant quarters and work rooms. He had told her once, it would not have surprised him if the room count of the family home was more than fifty.

After talking with her friend Katja still was not sure what a couple of words meant that he spoke about; Utility room, was one such word. Utility was the electric service company or gas company, not a room in the house. Did they have to have one room where all electrical appliances were stored or charged up? Then, how did they handle illumination of rooms? What was this closet? Was it a space only for the toilet? What is a den? And why would there be a garage in a home? A garage was where people took their automobiles to be repaired, but three of them in a home? How confusing?

Then, there was this SUV; what was that? But he had said nothing about the basement and the coal storage for heating the house. How really odd. Was there a heater in every room? Surely not, for she would have to be schlepping coal all day long to keep them going. Or were they wood stoves? She'd be splitting wood a lot for that. And yet he mentioned that the children could play inside the house and that their rooms were large enough to play in. So, they had to be heated. It was all so puzzling.

She had finally had the courage this one day to have Dimitri Gregorsky, her English teacher, read the letter and explain the questions she had. Dimitri had once been a minor official with the Security Police and had been allowed to travel abroad. He even spent some time in England before the collapse of the Soviet Union. But then something in his department went wrong, and they needed a scapegoat, and so Dimitri was sent into exile here in Novorotskoye. Then, with the collapse of the Communist regime in the early '90s, he was one of the forgotten flotsam. He was afraid to return to Moscow, for he had not served his time in Siberia, but the camp had been dismantled and so he worked at what he could and survived as best he could, as they all did.

Dimitri had read the letter and shaken his head. "I don't know, Katja," he had said. "But I can tell you one thing. Either this man is a very good agent, or all of this is honest. Somehow, I think this is all real. But I cannot answer your questions."

"You were overseas, right? So, tell me what you know?"

"Yes, I was abroad, several times even, but I was never allowed to live with the natives. I always had to live in the embassy compound and had to bunk with several other clerks, I did not even have my own private room. I did notice however, that the homes of the more well to do English people had garages attached to the houses to store their vehicles, when not in use. Usually, it was a small building in the back of the residence. It most often provided space for one car and very seldom for two. Only on the larger estates were there structures, where more than three or four cars could be housed, and these most often also contained living space for the chauffeur or some of the other servants of the estate. But he mentions no servants and no chauffeur, and why should he have need for more than one place to store his vehicle? I cannot answer these questions, Katja. I am so sorry.

"Katja, he mentions, that he will be sending you expense money, some of that in dollars. I would be very pleased, should you choose to pay me in that currency. You see, dear, Rubles are worth so very little, and I too have hopes of relocating somewhere outside the Russian borders. Even here, some items cannot be obtained without dollars. Even at the GUM in Moscow, you get better service and better-quality goods, if you can pay with dollars."

"I do not know how much he is sending, or how much I will need to get me there, but if I can spare any dollars, I will certainly let you have them." But to herself she thought, *only if I have more than I need after I give some to Tatiana and to Olga for emergency rations.* Cliff had sent more than sufficient funds, and she had been able to pay Dimitri in the desired currency.

After the lesson, Katja had gone to Tatiana. Together the women had talked over everything Katja had learned that day. It was a good day, because three of her outstanding paychecks had arrived. With them, she could cover all her expenses until she departed. So, on a whim she had invited Tatiana over for a feast. On their way to the dacha, Katja had splurged and bought a big pork roast and new potatoes and some fresh carrots, a tin of peas and very expensive fresh lettuce. At the bakery, they picked up dessert and a huge loaf of black bread to be shared with her friend. The women arrived at the dacha in an ebullient mood.

When Katja and her friend arrived back at the dacha, Oleg's horses and cart were waiting for him patiently by the door. He had given them some feed and filled a bucket with water for them, so Katja knew he was visiting with Olga and probably had already promised the children a ride around the village.

But when they entered the dacha, both Olga and Oleg came into the hall, all excited.

"You have a huge box from America. I put it in Olga's room so it does not get damaged, and wonder of wonders, it has not been searched by the KGB. Everything is intact. Come, come see!" Oleg pulled Katja by the hand.

"It is so big, it will take two of us to carry it upstairs. Olga did not want me to take it up for you before you returned home. You know Madame Bulin would be so nosey to open it, even before you came home."

Tatiana and Katja squeezed into Olga's room. The box was there. It was huge and took up all of the empty space in the middle of the room. One had to tiptoe around it.

Katja had looked at it. Sure enough, the sender was Cliff Collins of Boise City, Oklahoma, USA. She was leaving Russia. Why was he sending her stuff to take back? Just this morning, she had started on a list of items to pack to take with her to America and another of things to pack away and store for possible future shipments. She really had no travel trunks to accommodate such a large item. but Oleg hoisted the box and Olga opened the door to made sure the way was clear and every one trooped up to the attic.

On the way, they met the children coming out of Madame Bulin's rooms. An atmosphere of celebration ranged within the small crowd. No one living in the dacha had ever received such a large box. Everyone was excited to see what that enormous box contained. There was not enough space in her rooms to deposit the large container and so Oleg set it down gently in the attic space usually reserved for drying clothes. They all gathered around. There was suspense building as everyone was guessing what the box contained.

"Oleg, would you mind using your pocket knife and carefully slitting the seam open so not to destroy this good, large box? I might be able to store some of the things in it I need to leave behind."

Gently, he inserted the tip of his knife into the clear plastic wrapping tape and followed along the seam across the upper middle of the box, and he opened just as carefully the two side seams and stepped back so Katja could get down on her knees and open the container. Carefully, she lifted the four flaps, and there in front of her was a huge red suitcase. Taped to the middle of it was a large brown envelope. Katja removed the envelope. She looked inside; several items tumbled out of the envelope. There were several glossy pictures of a huge house. Then some odd looking little books fell into Katja's hands and several train tickets. Finally, she found a long letter. Laying all papers carefully aside, she took up the letter.

"You have to excuse me, friends. I need to read this letter first, so please be patient."

She unfolded the letter and read:

Dearest Ekatarina;

You make me so happy. I am delighted that you will come and join my life. Please tell the children hello from me and that I am excited to meet them

When your letter arrived a little over a week ago, I got very busy quickly to put everything into motion. First, I called my banker to order Rubles for me to send to you, but he told me that might be time consuming and difficult. It would be easier if I went down to Amarillo, Texas, to do that. He did get in contact with the President of First National Bank and got the ball rolling. So, the following day I went to Texas. I had several stops to make.

At the travel bureau, they helped me make your reservations on the trains and on the planes. So, included in this envelope are the train tickets for you and the children for your voyage. We got sleeping berths for you and the children for the train to Yekaterinburg, and also for the Trans-Siberian Train to Moscow. I am sorry, we were unable to get you a private compartment for the trip to Yekaterinburg. You will have a companion in that compartment, joining you about 10:00 A.M. for the remainder of that trip. I hope the person is pleasant. But at least no one will disturb your sleep for the first few hours of your travel. We could not get you a later departure time, so you and the children will have to depart your home town at 3:55 A.M.

The only other option I had was to make you spend a night in Yekaterinburg in a hotel. Since we had no good information on the availability of a hotel, we opted to have you leave so early in the day. But you have plenty of time in Yekaterinburg for supper and to change platforms.

I was able to obtain a private compartment for you on the train to Moscow. As the tickets show, you will leave your home on Thursday, November 26th. The train ride to Moscow will take three days. You will arrive Sunday evening, and you will depart Moscow Tuesday morning at 7:00 A.M. from Sheremetyevo Airport on an Aeroflot plane for London, England. There you will have to change planes and continue on an American Airlines plane to Dallas, Texas, USA. You will arrive in Dallas at 3:30 P.M. local time.

I will pick you up there. I will meet you, once you have cleared immigration and customs formalities. There is an area just outside that hall for passengers to be met. As soon as you clear that door, I will see you. I had hoped to help you through immigration, but that is not allowed. So, I will have to wait for you outside of that door.

You have reservations in Moscow at the Intourist Hotel. They are supposed to have an Airport Limousine and they are also to pick you up at the train station. I was told that this service is not too reliable so I have included funds, so you can take a taxi to get you around Moscow. Enjoy your free day in the big city. After the long train ride you will all be happy to have solid ground under your feet, I should think.

I have included 5000 Rubles. I hope that this is enough for all your expenditures. Do not bring any Rubles back with you, they are almost worthless anywhere else. Just in case I have included $1000.00 US also. In Moscow, they will accept them, and of course in London and on the planes. Except for porters and perhaps some drinks and snacks and maybe lunch in London, you should not have to spend any money. You should be served meals on the planes as well as on the trains. I have paid for all your meals in advance. You should not need very much; I think $100.00 US would be sufficient. But I do not want you to be short of funds, so I have included more than you should need, just in case.

The folks at the travel bureau advised me to send you suitcases approved by the Airlines. I expect you have plenty of things you would wish to bring with you. That is why I got you two of the largest cases available and for the children each a case they can handle. All cases have wheels and handles so they are easier to maneuver. You should check these at the airlines, but keep them with you on the trains. I have also included backpacks for each of you. Those you can store in the overhead compartments on the planes or under seat storage.

I have also included a fanny pack to keep all your important documents and your money in. Keep that around your waist inside your trousers, or under your sweater and coat, at all times. Thieves have a hard time removing that from your body. Every morning, put just enough money in your billfold so that you do not have to search for it in front of strangers and take only those tickets out you will need that day. You should be safe that way. There is also a satchel you can keep your purse and billfold in, which attaches easily to your suitcase.

You might like to keep a wet and a dry towel in it also. The wet towel can be kept in a plastic bag and you might like a small first aid kit and a little emergency sewing kit there. Also, any medications or headache remedies etc. should be kept close at hand. This advice comes from a friend who has experience traveling with small children. I have included small padlocks and keys for all suitcases. I do hope this makes your packing a little easier.

Don't bring along too many clothes. Bring just the changes you need during your journey and store those and some toys for the children in the backpacks. You should not have to open the suitcases during your voyage at all. However, you will most likely have to open them when you go through immigration. Do not bring any food along on the planes. You cannot take that into the country.

Dearest Katja, do not be upset with me. I went a little overboard while shopping for you and the children. I had so much fun and I have been told that light weight and warm clothing is hard to find in Russia. So, I found coats and hats, mittens and scarves for you all. I hope you like them and that they fit. I also bought trousers and sweaters for you. I bought some thermal underwear and T-shirts for all of you. I was told that it is already bitter cold in late November in your part of the world. Having no idea how well the trains are heated, I got them. If you do not need these items, give them to someone who can use them.

For the children, I bought some coloring books, crayons and some very small toys to keep them occupied while traveling. Please accept them in the spirit they were purchased. For you, there is a 35mm point and shoot automatic camera and twenty rolls of film. Please take pictures of everything and everyone you love from all angles. Bring the film back with you in the film safes. They will keep your pictures from being exposed as you go through airport security. Do not have them developed in Russia. I understand it is very expensive and not of the best quality.

Lastly, I have included a few snaps of the

house, since you seem to have a hard time picturing the place. The lady sitting on the porch is Inez Garza. She works for me keeping the house clean and Jorge her husband is my ranch hand. They live on the ranch in my old house. You will meet them. Inez is about your size. She promised to help you getting situated here.

Please let me know you received this parcel, so I can sleep without worrying so much.

I am so looking forward to picking you up in about three weeks in Dallas. I hope that this will find you and the children well. I can hardly wait for your arrival. Right now, I am in the process of redecorating the children's bedrooms with the help of my best friend and his wife. Take care and have a wonderful voyage. If you need anything else, call me. The number is 01 405 765 2345.

With my best wishes, and hoping for a comfortable voyage, I remain

Cliff

Katja's eyes were misting when she had finished reading the letter. Sasha saw it and was instantly worried that she was unhappy.

"No, son, these are happy tears."

"What's he say?" Everyone was clamoring and so Katja had read the letter out loud.

Tatiana put all their feeling succinctly into words.

"Katja, I think you are the most lucky woman in the world. I think this guy is very special. Let's see what he sent."

And so, with trembling hands she had lifted the first bright red suitcase out of the cardboard box. Beneath were two more smaller cases, exactly half the size and beneath that another bright red one. The cases were light, and Katja did not think anything was in them, but when she opened the first one, inside it she found a silver-grey coat. The garment was bulky but light and her size, she was sure. A colorful blue and white stockinet cap with matching muffler and knee high socks was there also.

There was a pair of silk lined black leather gloves lying beside them, and a package of the oddest underwear she had ever seen. The top was white with long sleeves printed with a small design of red and blue flowers. The underwear went all the way to the ankles in the same pattern. What she liked the most was a baby blue mohair and angora cowl neck sweater and gray wool pants.

"My God, those clothes are so beautiful. Just the right colors for you and so elegant. Katja, that man must be a prince." Tatiana whispered, and everyone nodded their head in agreement.

Irina's suitcase held underwear in pink, just like Katja's and a beautiful hot pink sweat suit with a white bunny nibbling on a flower on the front of the top. Her coat was a bright pink and her hat mittens and muffler had a colorful Scandinavian design to it. She too found warm matching woolen socks. Irina was clamoring to try everything on right away. Katja had to restrain her. She was dancing through the room hugging a white stuffed bunny.

Olga had remarked that she did not think she would ever have to worry about her little bird again. That man seemed to know how to take care of things.

For Sasha, there was a dark blue long coat jacket, and also a warm matching hat, mittens and a muffler and socks. For him, there were flannel lined jeans and a white Irish wool sweater that matched the hat, mittens and muffler. There was also plain white thermal underwear and a matching T-shirt.

He, too, had found a soft teddy bear, but being almost six years old and a big boy, he would not admit to wanting to cuddle that bear.

The last suitcase held the backpacks, matching in color their outerwear. In a side pocket of each was a matching thermos bottle. Then there were a small camera and those five film safes full of rolls of 35mm film and a large zippered tote containing the fanny pack pouch filled with money and tickets for the trains and planes and four small padlocks.

Lastly, in an envelope, Katja found four snap shots of a house. Everyone crowded around to have a look. The house seemed to be as big as the dacha, build of brick and stone with large windows and porches in front and back. There was outdoor furniture to be seen and a tiny woman was sitting on what seemed to be a swing for two people. They all commented that it was highly unlikely that no one else lived in such a large dwelling, but it sure was a nice-looking place.

While the adults had admired the photographs, the children had examined their backpacks and discovered a thick coloring and activity book in each and a box of Crayolas. Sasha had found six matchbox cars, and Rina had found a small Barbie doll and a small trunk filled with the doll's clothing.

Everyone was talking at the same time. Soon, the children would be hungry, and Katja had not started with the dinner preparations. Oleg was talking earnestly with Sasha, and Olga was crying, saying with a man like that around, her little bird would soon forget her. Tatiana mused that perhaps she, too, should look for an American man to marry. Surely, there would be more like him. Rina had heard the remark and quite earnestly injected into the conversation

"No, my Papi is special. I told Mama and Sacha that when I first saw his picture. There is no one like him at all."

Sadly, Tatiana answered: "I think you might be right, Little Bird. I think you are all very lucky."

"Yes," the little girl said quite solemnly.

Finally, Katja was able to move the things from the big box into her rooms. She needed to prepare dinner, for soon it would be time for the children to go to sleep. She knew, however, that this day, they were too excited and would probably want to stay up for a long time.

Olga and Tatiana helped her prepare their feast and Oleg entertained the children, and he made sure that all her gifts found their way into her rooms. The empty box he stored near the door to her rooms, so no one could abscond with it.

It was too late to cook a roast that evening, but Katja decided they could cut pork chops out of the meat, which would cook that much faster, and Olga offered to take half down to her rooms and cook them there, so they all could eat together and not in shifts. She brought up a bottle of vodka for a celebration after dinner and for breaking in the new camera. Katja was able to take many pictures of her friends that evening.

Katja remembered that the days flew past, as she made preparations for her departure from Russia. Two weeks hardly seemed enough time, she remembered. But it was good too, that she had so little time, for it left less time for second thoughts or for becoming too nervous. She was so busy these last few weeks, she never had time to think. Now, Katja tried to remember when she did what, and only two months later, it was impossible to remember it all. That brought her to thinking about the dacha and her two rooms up in the attic. Could she still remember it all perfectly? Probably, but which space had her father's picture occupied? To the left of the little inkpot, or to the right, or was that where her mother's picture had been? She chastised herself for being so forgetful, or had she moved those pictures around a bit, when dusting? Probably.

Still she was sad for forgetting so soon. Was it because she was so happy here that she had forgotten some of the details so quickly? Was it that Russia did not matter anymore? No, it mattered, she was sure of that. It had shaped her into the person she was now. *So, think Katja, and always remember it all,* she mentally exhorted herself.

Chapter Twelve

Christmas was moving inexorably closer. Cliff was behaving oddly. One day he was gone most of the day, and when he returned home late that evening, he asked her, to make sure that the children would not enter the barn and especially not the tack room, and then he winked at her and grinned from ear to ear. What was all that about? Katja could not understand his behavior. He knew the children would never enter the barn without him being with them. And why the wink and grin? If he knew they were good, why even make such a request? The next morning, there were quite a number of gaily wrapped boxes under the tree. Where had they come from? One tiny one was exquisitely and elegantly wrapped. Cliff forbade everyone to touch the packages until Christmas day.

The next time Inez came to do the cleaning, she asked Katja what she was going to give Cliff as a present? Katja was taken aback. She had to give him a present? She did not know about that. What could she give him? She could not go to the store alone; besides, he had everything and she had no money. She stuttered, telling Inez she thought Christmas was just for children, not for adults. It is, she was reassured, but one always gives a present or two to the important people in one's life. She herself was going to give Jorge a new pair of jeans and a nice flannel cowboy shirt. All this information put Katja in a panic. Her worry increased when Inez told her she knew that Cliff had bought her something very special.

A few days later, when Donna Brewer came over, she too asked what she was going to give Cliff and offered to take her to town shopping. At the same time, Donna wanted to know if they had set the wedding date. Katja told her that most likely they would go to the Justice of the Peace in town the week between Christmas and New Year's. But no specific day had been reserved. They would get married, when they both had the time to spare to go to town. She was not overly concerned. Donna informed her that would never do.

"We have to set the day, get you your gown and trousseau and make reservations for the party and your honeymoon. I'll take care of the kids, or Inez will, but you'll have a proper wedding and honey moon. No question about that. Now" she said to Katja "Do you have your gown and all?"

"What gown is that? No special dress is

needed. I wear beautiful new pants and nice blue sweater Cliff gave me."

"No, after Christmas you and I will go to Amarillo and we will get you all fixed up."

When Cliff came in from the barn Donna asked him "When's the wedding? The six weeks is almost up."

"We figured on going down to the court house and getting hitched the week after Christmas, so I can claim them all on my income tax this year."

"Clifford Collins, this woman is not an income tax deduction. Forget about that for this year. She is your bride and as such she deserves a proper wedding. And she is going to have one, just like Mary did, and Don and I are going to stand up with you before the priest. Just like we did the last time. You are not running down to the court house to get hitched, like someone is pointing a shotgun at your arse. No, the most eligible bachelor in the county is going to have a shindig like he deserves. Is that understood? And then you are going to take your bride on a honeymoon for a week, without kids, and dogs and worries about the ranch. I'll take the kids, and Jorge is quite capable of seeing to the ranch in winter. I'll take Katja to Amarillo and we'll get her dress and shoes and vail and the whole outfit. Now, don't you fret none about this, or I'll call Don to talk some sense into you. Now, let me see a calendar."

All Cliff could say was "Yes mam, and here is your calendar."

"Okay, let me see now. Christmas eve is on a Friday, that makes the first of January on a Saturday. You'll get married the following Friday at the club. I'll take Katja to Amarillo on Wednesday before New Year's and see that she has a haircut at the same time. Trina at the beauty shop can set her hair for the wedding, but she can't cut it, she'd botch it for sure. Katja, what religion are you?"

"Religion, I do not know. In Russia, no religion, although, now, some of the older people go back to church, Orthodox I think. Is what my father was as a child. He taught me a little. But I never been to a church. There once was one in our little town, but Communists made a bar out of it. It still has a little steeple and a bell. There was talk in the village of making it a church again, if they can find a priest, and if they can find another place for the bar."

"That's going to be tough. There is no Russian orthodox church here in town, not even a Greek orthodox church. I think there is one in Amarillo. Cliff, go call right now. See if you can get one of their preachers here on that first Friday of the year. That would be good."

Cliff again said "Yes ma'am" and walked up

to his office to make several phone calls. When he came down an hour later, he was smiling the biggest smile ever.

"I found us a priest and he is willing to come up here on Thursday and work with the Catholic priest here in town, and we'll get married in the Church here and then we can have the party at the club, a dinner and all. You had a great idea, Donna. When you and Katja go to Amarillo next week, you'll stop by the church and visit with the priest for just a few minutes. He wants to get know the bride at least too. He wants to talk to her for a few minutes. I'll stop by tomorrow; I have to go to town on a few errands anyhow."

"Do you have a tux? It might be good to get a silver grey one. Get fitted and a light blue cumber bund".

"Anything else, Miss Boss?"

"Let me think about that, I'll let you know."

Katja had been watching the debate and grew more and more worried. She did not know, what all this going on about the wedding, was about. She and Sergey had one day decided they might as well get married and gone to the Justice Palace paid their 10 Rubles and were married. Tatiana and his friend Boris had gone later with them to the one restaurant in town, where they had dinner and a few drinks and that was their wedding. No special dress, no special shoes and what is a tux and this cumber bund?

Besides, there was the worry about this present for Christmas. How was she going to do that? Sasha saw her being troubled and asked what was wrong and in Russian she whispered her fears to him. Irina joined in the conversation.

"Is no problem, Mama", she pronounced. "Just give him that one big ring, that you said Grandpapa wore all the time. Is pretty and I know my Papi would like it." Then she added that she was painting a big picture for her Papi for her gift to him. Sasha too, wanted him to have something they brought from Russia.

"Let's look at some of the things you have in the suitcases that you forgot to show Mr. Cliff. There must be something we could give him."

"Yes, I just had an idea. You are very good, my children. Thank you, for helping me."

Just then she heard Donna say to Cliff.

"I think Katja and I will come along tomorrow with you. We can all visit with the priest, and afterwards you can drop us off at the mall while you do your errands and pick us up later. Let's call Inez to make sure she can handle the kids for tomorrow." And so, it was all arranged.

They left for Amarillo at seven in the morning and met with the Orthodox priest first. To Katja's surprise, he knew a little Russian, and he was able to ask her in private, if she really wanted this marriage, or if she was being bullied into it. Once he was convinced that Katja really wanted to marry Cliff, he went ahead planning the ceremony, and he was able to explain the whole affair to her. He spoke to each of them privately for a few minutes, and then invited all for the conversation about the ceremony. He was also able to tell them, that the Catholic priest had given permission for them to use his church. He had already been able to arrange that, after he had talked with Cliff on the phone the previous day.

The priest had agreed to have the wedding ceremony after his morning services where over. Ten in the morning seemed like a good time for the ceremony to begin. They would have the rest of the day for the party.

He even suggested to include the children in the ceremony, Irina as flower girl and Aleksandr as ring bearer. It would be good for them psychologically, to see their mother pledged to her new husband. Being included, would also give them a feeling of a united family and belonging to the new husband. Katja laughed at that. The priest looked questioning at her, and she had to explain how little Irina had called Cliff her papi the first time she had seen his picture, and he had not disappointed the little girl. He doted on her as much as she doted on him.

Although Sasha was more reserved, he had accepted Cliff fully and had just within the last few days started to call him papi too, on a few occasions.

Afterwards, they all had an early lunch to which they invited the priest. He accepted and so for the occasion, they went to the Amarillo Country Club, where Cliff was holding a reciprocal membership.

Afterward, the ladies went shopping and Cliff returned the priest to his home and ran the errands, he had wanted to come to the city for in the first place. He picked up the ladies around four in front of the Macy's store where Katja had purchased her wedding gown, vail, shoes and hat. They had also purchased a light blue frilly dress or Irina and a pair of long pants and a dark coat and baby blue cumber bund for Sasha as well as a white dress shirt and a little bow tie.

Before leaving town, they all went to the Kroger Supermarket to pick up groceries for the holidays. Katja was surprised, when she realized, how much food they needed. Was it only a little over two weeks since they had been to the store?

She would have to learn to keep a much closer eye on the groceries in the future, so she should not have to go so often, Katja realized once they started to shop. Donna told her not to worry.

"It took me years to learn all the ins and outs. Next month, when you're back from your honeymoon you and I will go together. Then you can ask me, what do with some of the stuff they sell, and I'll show you some ways to make do without having to run into town so often. I had help when I was a young wife, and Cliff's Mary had his grandmother to teach her all she must know. Neither of us had children the first couple of years of our marriage. Kids really add another dimension to the shopping experience.

"Summer makes it even harder, for it will be difficult to get some of the stuff home before it defrosts. Let me tell you, shopping in July, August and September is an art." Katja was showing concern and she looked downright scared. "Ah, don't let me scare you. We have ways to overcome the problems and challenges. It's easier now than ever."

"Oh, before I forget it, let me remind you, to pick up baking supplies. Or have you baked all your Christmas cookies already?" Donna had changed the subject a bit.

"No, what is this? I did not know about baking special cookies. Will you give me your recipe, please?

"You don't have to bake special cookies. But in my family, we always have. We make a big plate full of different cookies for everyone to munch on all day long. It was something my mom did for us kids, and to me, it's just not Christmas without the special treats, we get only at Christmas time, like decorated sugar cookies, and Lebkuchen, Speculatius,

Pfeffernuesse and Dominosteine." Cliff interrupted her by saying.

"Mary always bought all those cookies at that special bakery in town here. We'll go by there and see if they have some. But it would be nice if you could make just a few batches Katja. The house always smells so wonderful when Christmas cookies are being baked." Cliff confided.

"Don't worry about baking a bunch of cookies, my kids liked to help decorate them. It was a ritual at our house and I'll give you all my recipes. I'm sure your little ones will want to help also."

"Now then, to change the subject, have you two decided, where you want to go on your honeymoon?" Cliff answered that.

"Katja wanted to see palm trees when she first landed. They have them down in San Antonio and Austin and on the coast. But I'm thinking the coast is nasty this time of year. Even New Orleans is not such a fun city in the winter. There is plenty to do though in San Antonio and we could go down through the hill country and stop off in some of those towns that are so much fun, like Fredericksburg and Wimberley, but again, it's winter."

"Have you all thought about New Mexico? Santa Fe or Taos are fun places even in winter. But of course, no palm trees. The plus side there is, it won't take you two days hard driving to get there. Unless you want to take her to Tulsa or Oklahoma City?"

"Na, we'll go to the City for the Commissioners Safety meetings in March and if we have the time, we can run up to Tulsa too. They always schedule lots of stuff for the families to do, while we're in meetings. The kids would like that too, like the zoo and the Cowboy Hall of Fame and maybe riding the boats down on the river, Frontier City, you know all that stuff." He continued.

"I kind of like your idea of going to Santa Fe, Donna. There is so much art and shopping there, and the museums and good restaurants. Yea, staying at La Fonda or the Inn of the Governors or even the Bishops Lodge might be great fun. From there we could take day trips all around, and the town is so different from most American towns. Yes, she might like that a whole lot. I'll check on it tomorrow."

"Why is that city different from other towns?" Katja asked.

"It is the oldest capital city in the U. S. But it's history and culture and architecture is totally different from other towns and States. New Mexico is kind of unique, simply because it was for most of its history a province of Mexico and belonged to Spain in the beginning. It is the one State where people speak Spanish as well as English. It only became a State in 1943, even after Oklahoma became a State and a hundred years after Texas became a State. You'll find most of the chain stores there, but even they have to conform to Santa Fe architecture. Then the town is high up in the mountains. There is a ski resort right outside of town. Same with Taos and then there are the pueblos all over."

"What is pueblos, please, explain to me?"

"They are the homes, villages of indigenous people. Some of them are over a thousand years old. All of them are from before white people arrived here in the south west."

"Indigenous people? Don't they live in tents? Like our Mongols?"

"No, not these, they live in stone houses. Some of them are inside huge caves and build of stone, others are made of a kind of mud brick, called adobe. It is all very different. I can't explain it. I'll show you some pictures when we get home."

"I did not know that. You must teach me about indigenous people, Indians, yes? I was taught they live in tents made of leather and long poles and all ride horses."

"There were people like that. Some still have a teepee for special occasions. They all live in regular houses now. Some still have horses for enjoyment, but all have cars and trucks, just like we do."

"There are no indigenous people here or in Boise City. They were never here, right?"

"Oh yes, there were plenty here, Apache and Comanche, and Sioux. I am sure that there is a family or two of Native Americans, who live in Boise City and lots of them are in Amarillo. Palo Duro Canyon is just outside of Amarillo. That was a very important place for the plains tribes. Many of them wintered in the canyon. And the high plains were their hunting grounds, for that is where the buffalo lived. That was their most important game. Amarillo and Boise City have been built on the high plains."

"Not here, not where we live?"

"Oh yes, they lived here. When spring comes, I will show you some old camping places right on our ranch, where the Natives camped for long times. You can still see where they had their camp fires and you can see where the teepee poles where set in the ground. And not far away is a big pile of buffalo bones. I keep the cattle and horses out of the area, for I think our history should be preserved. There is even a small stretch, where the Santa Fe cut off trail crossed our land not very far from the house. I'll show it to you the next time we are out and about."

"Oh yes, please. Show me and the children, and tell them all about this indigenous people."

"I think I will invite Robert Yellow Bird and

his wife some evening, and let them tell you about their people, their customs. I don't feel that I know enough, and then I might tell you some of the things, we Europeans believe erroneously."

"Thank you. I think that will be very educational for us all."

While discussing all this, they had slowly wound their way along the aisles of the supermarket, and their shopping cart was once again filled to the brim. Donna's cart too was loaded to overflowing.

She laughed, "I always find it incomprehensible, how two people can put so much food away in no time. In two weeks, I'll find myself again with a mostly empty larder. No matter how much I bring home, by next week's end, I'll start running short on something, and by the end of the second week, I will have a list a mile long of what I need. So, Katja, don't feel bad, when you get home and find out you forgot to buy something important."

"How you remember what to buy?"

"The first thing I do at home, once I have put all this stuff up, is I take a big sheet of lined paper and put it up on my fridge with a pencil attached on a long string. Every time I run low on something, it goes on the list. I divide my list into a food shopping list and an etc. list, for everything else: like nails, or duct tape, writing paper, sewing thread, buttons for his shirts, vacuum cleaner bags. You know, all the incidentals you forget, if you don't write them down.

I cross out the items as I put them in my cart or purchase them, and I check more than once that I have everything on that list. You know, as I get older, it gets harder and harder to remember everything. You can't laugh it off as a senior moment when you are 100 miles from the store and you need B-B-Q Sauce for the steaks you are grilling." She laughed more, "Without my lists, I would be unable to function."

"I think is good idea, yes. Must learn to make lists, too." Katja was serious. "I never had to buy for more than two days at a time. Much easier if you forget something. Pick it up the next day on your way home. No problem."

They had arrived at the checkout counter. Unbeknownst to the women, Cliff had filled a second basket with lots of incidentals that Katja had not even thought about. He had gotten juicy tangerines and a huge bag of mixed nuts for cracking and a couple of bags of marshmallows for roasting in the fire. He had seen a beautiful Christmas cactus in full bloom.

Then there were the baking supplies Katja had not thought about: almonds and a couple of boxes of candied fruit for Stollen and walnuts and pecans for pies, heavy cream for whipping and a couple of small bottles of vanilla extract and pumpkin spice, and two big bags of ten pounds of all-purpose flour, yeast, baking powder and powdered sugar and brown sugar and another bag of granulated sugar, food coloring and spritzels for decorating cookies. He looked sheepish, when Katja looked aghast.

"I just remembered all the stuff my grannie had me buy for her holiday baking. Besides, if Donna had another senior moment, we can help her out." He laughed hard, and Katja smiled. Donna, however. was not so amused.

As soon as all the groceries had been stored in the big SUV, Cliff took the ladies to dinner, and then it was time to drive home to the ranch. On the way, a lot of the particulars about the wedding were ironed out. Katja, however, was still puzzled about the cookie baking. She could not figure out if it all had been a joke, or if she actually was expected to be baking mountains of cookies. In the end, she decided to bake lots of cookies and let the children help her decorate a few of the ones for which she would roll out the dough and then cut out. She had found the tin containing several cookie cutters Cliff had secreted in his cart.

They arrived back home at the ranch in good spirits. Still, it was hard for Katja to understand all the fuss about the wedding and about Christmas.

Chapter Thirteen

After breakfast the following day, Katja started baking. She looked at the recipes from Donna and Inez. She started on a simple recipe: sugar cookies. Rina wanted to help doing the actual mixing of the batter, but at this time that was not possible. Katja had her daughter hand her the eggs, then the butter, and finally the cup filled with sugar. Although the little one was trying to be careful, she spilled a little of the sugar. Katja refilled the measuring cup.

By lunchtime, they had baked several batches of cookies. Katja promised the children that they could decorate the cookies after they had lunch and had taken their naps. Again, they tried to weasel out of taking that nap, but they knew better, once they had eaten, they trooped off to their rooms without further ado.

At lunchtime, Cliff came in smiling, "Oh, God, how this reminds me of the old days, when my grandmother used to bake cookies for Santa Claus." He came right up to Katja and gave her a big hug and a smooch. "Thank you so much, Sweetheart. This will be the best Christmas ever."

While the children were decorating during the afternoon, Katja found some of the recipes she had brought from Russia. The recipes had come from her father, who seemed to have had them from his mother or the cook at the estate in Russia. The smells brought back faint memories also. Somewhere in her past, there was a memory of someone baking during long winter days. Had her mother done that? Or was it Olga who used to bake, when she was a little girl? She remembered tasting the little rocks filled with fruit, raisins, nuts and such. The cookies had been drenched with powdered sugar. She remembered feasting on those wonderful morsels. Now, she was trying to bake them here in America.

Christmas was magical. Christmas eve, Cliff asked that the children go to bed on time, so that Santa might come during the night and leave his presents for them. He also asked the children to put out a plate of cookies and a glass of milk, for a snack for Santa. He even went and got a big bowl of sweet feed for the reindeer. He winked at Katja as he made all these preparations. Finally, after the children had been asleep for quite some time, and he was sure of it, he told Katja that he was going to out to the barn to get some things in. She could not understand what he was talking about, were not all of the presents already under the tree? She was sure nothing more could be placed beneath that tree. There could not possibly be anything else that he could have gotten for the children. They had so many things now. Anything else was just not possible

.

While in Amarillo that last time, he had also asked her to purchase some small presents for her friends in Russia, especially for the Sasha's friend Sergey. She had been surprised by his generosity towards her friends. She had shipped a large box with clothes the children had already outgrown to Sergey and his sister, and her own coat, she had shipped to her friend Tatiana. She had included pictures of her new home and of some of the sights in Dallas, such as the ice rink in the shopping mall and some of those awful road intersections. She had also taken pictures of the flowers blooming in Dallas and of the holiday decorations of the homes she had seen. She had included some warm clothing for Olga and for Oleg.

Hopefully, everything would arrive on or before Epiphany, the day, when people in old Russia had celebrated the arrival of the wise men with giving gifts to one another. She hoped her few presents would be welcomed by her friends.

When Cliff finally joined her in the bedroom, he brought along hot chocolate and a few cookies to snack on, before they, too, would try to get a little sleep before morning arrived and made any more rest impossible. He was as excited as the children were, and she knew, he would be up long before first light, anticipating the children's excitement.

She was right, Cliff was up by 5:00 A.M. and padded softly into the living area to light the tree, again and to make more hot chocolate and snatch another few cookies, and then he sat in his recliner, awaiting developments. He did not have to wait long; the children were up long before their normal time for getting up in the mornings. It was still dark outside. Rina's shriek of surprise is what wakened Katja. The little one came rushing into the bedroom, all excited.

"Mami and Papi, you have to come and see what the Claus man left us. There is oh, so much, I can't see it all, and you have to tell Sasha to come too. Come, Mami, you have to see; and the cookies and the milk and the reindeer food is all gone, too. He really came and found us, it is so unbelievable. Come!" She was pulling her mother out of the bed.

"Irina, I have to get dressed first, before I go out there. So please, be patient. Your Papi too is still asleep. Take it easy, and please be quiet. Your Papi needs his rest."

"No, I am awake, and you don't need to get

dressed now; just put on your robe. Everyone does that, when they get up so early in the morning. I bet Sasha will be awake any moment now. Come, let's have some more hot chocolate."

When Katja walked into the living room, she was surprised that the tree was lit. She was sure, she had unplugged the lights before going to bed last night. And the area around the tree was filled with presents. There were so many, some were hidden behind the others, and so Katja could not ascertain what all was hidden there.

Sasha came out of his room, still in his sleepers, tired looking and tussle haired.

"Is it morning already? I am still so sleepy," and then he saw the tree and the mountain of presents. "Oh, Mama, he really did come and leave us presents."

Katja made hot cholate for everyone, while Cliff found Christmas music on his CDs. He made them all sing with the music for a little while, and finally he suggested, "Sasha, would you be so kind and hand out the presents, there are names on all the packages. You can read them, right?"

"Yes, I can do that. Is that permissible, or does everyone pick out their own presents?"

"I think it would be too chaotic, if we all

scrambled under the tree. You just hand out one present at the time and wait for that present to be opened, before you hand out another one. Can you do that?"

"Yes, Mr. Cliff, Papi."

"I wonder who all these presents are for. Surely, they are not all for you two. There is far too much here for just the two of you." Katja was trying to dampen the enthusiasm.

"No, most of the packages are for you all, but there are a few for our friends. If you cannot read the name, give the packages to me, and I will tell you who they are for. Okay?" Cliff was giving more instructions to Sasha.

"Find my present first, Sasha. I want to know what that Santa Claus has left for me." Irina was certain that there was something for her.

"Have you been a good girl all year? Santa only leaves presents for good children. Bad children get a piece of coal in their packages," Cliff told the children, to heighten the suspense.

"There have been times when I thought you were not very good, Rina." Katja reminded her daughter.

"I have been good." The little girl stated, but a

shadow of doubt crossed her face and Sasha was suddenly a bit fearful.

The first package he picked up, was for Cliff. It was a nice warm plaid shirt that Katja had found in the store in Amarillo, the day they had shopped for her bridal gown. Next, there was a package for Sasha. It was quite heavy and when he opened it, he found a big book of Russian fairy tales in English. Soon, he would have to learn to read more than what he was able to do now.

Next, came a picture book with simple words for his sister, and then Sasha found the small package, that was so beautifully wrapped, the one they all had admired for several days now. Cliff asked him, to give the little box to him and then Cliff went down on his knees in front of Katja as he handed the package to her. She opened it and was speechless. Inside a little red velvet-covered box was a beautiful ring.

"Will you please marry me, Katja? This is a little token of my affection and my promise to marry you, if you will have me."

Katja looked stunned; tears were forming in her eyes and she smiled the biggest smile the children had ever seen on her and gave Cliff a big hug and kiss and told him, that she would like nothing more than to be his wife.

There were endless numbers of gifts. Finally,

towards the back, behind all the other packages, Sasha unearthed a bicycle with training wheels for himself and a red tricycle for his sister.

He had also discovered a baby carriage with a doll for Irina and a dollhouse for all her furniture. Sasha too had received a barn for all his farm animals. The item that puzzled him the most was the saddle, just his size, he found under the tree.

"Now I can really help Mr. Cliff Papi and ride one of the horses, when he goes out to check the fences. I can go with him." Turning to Cliff, he asked "May I ride Buttercup, when you ride fence? I think this saddle will fit her too, and she likes me, I think. Please Mr. Cliff, Papi?"

"I don't see why not. Perhaps, though, we might find you a horse that will fit you a little better? One that is exactly your size. Would you like that, Sasha? Maybe for your birthday, we'll get you your own horse? How would that be?"

"I do not think that is necessary, Mr. Cliff. There are so many horses here already. Surely one of them would be suitable for Sasha?" Katja interjected. She felt the child had more than enough presents already, and to her a horse was an impossible expense.

"You think, I might someday have my own horse? No, a boy could not ask for such, and I already have that cowboy hat and the saddle. Surely, I could not ask for more." But a wistful, expectant smile covered his face.

Finally, all the presents under the tree had been distributed. The mountain of presents besides each of their places was indeed huge, and the mountain of discarded wrapping paper was even greater. There was, however, still one present they had not found yet. It would be the greatest surprise for Sasha and was not waiting under the tree. Once all the gifts had been distributed, Cliff asked them all to come out to the barn with him. There, in a stall was a small pony, the first steed for Sasha. Aleksandr was speechless. A small horse, all for him. Now, he could really help Mr. Cliff, when he was riding fence, or breaking ice, or even taking out feed to the horses. The little guy was so happy that he did not know what to do. His first riding lesson would be later that day.

There were still a few presents left under the tree for their friends, for Inez and Jorge and their family and for Don and Donna. All these people came over later in the day and brought small gifts for everyone. Katja felt so helpless. She had not thought to get anything for these people. She thought the holiday was just for the children. She could not comprehend that you bought things for all the people you cared about.

Two days later, both she and her son wrote letters back to their friends in Russia. Even little Irina got in on the act and had her write a note to Olga.

Sasha's letter to his friend Sergey was once again dictated and written by his mother.

Sergey;

Christmas was two days ago. Santa Claus came and brought us all so many presents. Irina now has more toys than all the children in Novorotskoye combined.

You won't believe it, but I am now a real cowboy, just like Walker on television. I have my own cowboy hat and a saddle, but best of all, I have my own horse. Yes, I have my own horse! He is a little pony, and I named Billie. I have had some riding lessons already, and soon I will be able to help Mr. Papi with the chores. I don't even have to walk to the barn. No, I can ride my new silver and blue bicycle to the barn or down to Jorge's house. I never have to walk anymore. My bicycle has training wheels. Mr. Papi has promised to remove them, once I am able to ride more confidently.

Rina, too, received a tricycle from Santa Claus. Her bike is red, and she likes to ride it on the walkways around the house. There are no rocks in the way, that way. All the walks are smooth concrete paths. And she has a doll house for all her furniture, and a baby carriage and a new big baby doll. Please tell Olga Kerchenova that we are all so very happy.

I must close this letter, for I have to go and take care of Billie, my horse. Please write me a letter and tell me if you got the presents we sent you.

I sure wish you were here. We could have so much fun riding my horse together.

I miss you so much.

Alexandr

Irina too wanted a letter send to her friend Olga. In it, she told of all the wonderful things Santa Claus brought her. She described her new room minutely and included a couple of pictures to show Olga what her room looked like. She also included a picture of the mountain of presents under the tree and of all the wrapping paper that was being discarded. She told Olga to come and visit. She could sleep with her in her princess room or even in the spare bedroom upstairs.

After she had finished with the letter, she finally asked her mother if it was permissible for Olga to come to visit for a day or two.

Katja too, wrote a letter to her friend Tatiana, describing all the festivities on Christmas and the surprises she and the children had received.

She told her of her impending wedding and the beautiful gown she had obtained for a fairy wedding, just like you see on television from America. She told Tatiana of her planned honeymoon in Santa Fe and described much of what she had learned about the town and the State of New Mexico. She confessed she was still bewildered by all the hullabaloo about the wedding.

She also confided that it made her feel wonderful, that everyone was going out of their way for her and to make sure her wedding would be festive and memorable. She promised to send pictures of the wedding and of her gown. She confessed she was bewildered by all the preparations. Even a priest would be coming all the way from Amarillo for her wedding. Her children too, would be included in the ceremony. Can you imagine such an affair? Those were her last remarks to her friend.

New Year's Eve came and with it a party at the club. Everyone was there, and the occasion was quite festive. Katja had been surprised when Cliff asked her to dress up and even wear some of her jewelry. He explained he wanted his future wife to shine. The children were entertained that evening by Amanda, the Garza's youngest daughter. Katja had never experienced such a gathering. At midnight, the club had all the guests go out and watch a fireworks show. After a final toast to greet the New Year, everyone went home.

Chapter Fourteen

The wedding was scheduled for the fifth of January. The church ceremony took place in the old Catholic church with the minister of the Russian Orthodox Catholic Church of Amarillo, Texas, performing the ceremony and the priest of the Roman Catholic Church of Boise City, assisting.

Katja looked lovely in the new white gown, with the veil hiding her from all. Cliff looked distinguished in his silver-grey tux with the baby blue cumber bund. The stars of the ceremony, however were two little urchins. Irina wore that frilly baby blue dress and carried a bouquet of lily of the valley and forget me nots and Aleksandr wore long light grey pants and a baby blue shirt and a navy blazer.

Katja could not understand all the fuss. She and Sergey had just gone down to the Hall of Justice on a day when they both had the afternoon off and afterward had a nice dinner and a bit of vodka with a few friends.

Why this huge affair, and what was the significance of the white gown and the veil? But she did feel festive and special. Cliff even advised that she wear some of her grandmother's jewels and the tiny coronet to hold her veil in place. A photographer was dogging their every step and taking pictures of everything, but the priest had been right; the children felt very special, to be included in the ceremony. Besides being the ring bearer, Sasha was even called upon to walk his mother up the aisle, and in essence, give her away. And little Irina was her mother's best maid with the assistance of Donna, the wife of Cliff's best friend.

Afterwards, there was a huge dinner and dance. Towards late afternoon, the bride and groom left the party in progress, to change into traveling clothes for the drive to Santa Fe, in New Mexico. They had reservations at the Bishops Lodge, a gift from Don and Donna. The children would be taken care of by Inez and her daughter Amanda.

There was snow on the ground once they reached the outskirts of Raton, but Interstate 25 was free of the white stuff.

They arrived at their hotel just before it was time for the kitchen to close. Dinner was scrumptious and so different from any food with which Katja was familiar. New Mexican fare presented a whole different cuisine, different from anything she had ever eaten.

"Oh, that was good, but, oh, so spicy. I think my throat is on fire. I must learn to make these dishes."

So, the next day, while exploring the "City Different" they bought Katja a new cookbook featuring the cuisine of New Mexico. To help with that, Cliff obtained several *ristras* of Hatch peppers. Katja was enchanted with the town. She had visited Dallas and Fort Worth and some of the suburbs, also Wichita Falls and Amarillo.

Those towns were all similar, but Santa Fe, truly, is a different town. The architecture is so unique, and that the town is older than any other in the States seemed hard to comprehend. The town is even older than many of the towns in old Russia. That came as complete news to Katja.

They shopped on the square, Cliff buying her turquoise and silver jewelry. Katja finally asked if it would be permissible if they were to pick up some trinkets for both Donna and Inez, who had helped her so much, and a pair of dangly earrings for her friend Tatiana, who had sold her last pair of earrings for a new pair of work shoes. Cliff was happy to consent.

Katja loved the mountains. Here were places that reminded her of home. Even the trees looked familiar. Homesickness attacked her on the drive over the high road to Taos on their last day in town. The little villages they came through, reminded her a little of her home town of Novorotskoye. She was totally happy in New Mexico and had Cliff promise her to bring her again.

They arrived home at the end of six very happy days. The children seemed not to have missed them at all, but they were happy to have them back, of course. Everyone loved the small gifts they had picked up for them. Rina was excited about the little earrings Cliff had bought for her, unbeknownst to her mother. Sasha was surprised to receive a Bolo tie, similar to the one Mr. Cliff Papi wore, when he got dressed to go to town. Rina too, received a little bangle for her wrist.

"Cliff, you spoil them too much. The children just got all those presents at Christmas, and now you have things for them again. He had gotten a bear claw necklace for Sasha, and for both of the children he had bought books about the lives of Native American children.

A letter from Russia was waiting for them when they returned from their honeymoon. The letter was written by Katja's friend Tatiana, but all of her friends had contributed to it. They all thanked her for the presents they had received and for the pictures she had included. They marveled at her good fortune, could not imagine having to drive those roads in Texas, could not believe that flowers were blooming, when snow made any kind of outside activity almost impossible in their part of the world. Sergey and Elena, the children's friends, had been impressed by the pictures of the Tarrant County Court House, and Sergey was envious of Sasha's adventures there. Olga and Tatiana were astounded by the size of Katja's new home. They could not fathom all the new appliances she was describing. Everyone told her she was the luckiest woman on the planet.

But the letter brought a bit of homesickness to the immigrants. Katja immediately sat down and penned a return letter, telling her friends of her wedding and honeymoon. She included pictures of the event and of the town of Santa Fe. She also sent the earrings they had purchased for Tatiana and the little silver and turquoise cross for Olga and a money clip for Oleg. Katja felt like crying when she was finished with the letter. She missed her friends so much, but there was no question of her ever returning to Russia. No, she was in the United States for good, and she was totally happy here. She dried her tears and looked on the bright side. She realized it was only her friends she missed, not the town or Russia or her two rooms in the dacha.

Chapter Fifteen

It was during the third week of January that they had some rather unwelcome visitors. Late in the afternoon, the doorbell sounded. Cliff had just come in from seeing after county business. He was still in the shower when two gentlemen appeared at the front door. They asked to come in and asked for Cliff. The children were still taking their naps. Katja was apprehensive. She did not invite them into the living room, but had them stand in the entrance hall while she got Cliff.

"Who is it, Katja?"

"I don't know. I have never seen them. They look mean."

Still in his T-shirt and jeans, drying his hair,

Cliff followed her into the hall.

"Hey, Bill, Dave. What's up? What brings you here today? Come have a seat. You all need something to drink?"

"This is not a social visit, Cliff. We are here as truant officers for the school district."

"What on earth for?"

"It has come to our attention that you have children living here and that they are not enrolled in school, as is the law."

"You have got to be kidding me. My wife's children are too young to be enrolled in school. Besides, they do not speak enough English to go to a public school. We were going to keep her son here at home and teach him until the fall, when he is six years old."

"How old are those children now?"

"Irina is three, and Aleksandr is five. Neither are school age yet."

"That is where you are wrong. Both those kids need to be in school, and we have teachers to teach them English. there are enough Mexicans in Boise City, for us to have a language teacher. That boy needs to be in first grade, or at least in Kindergarten, and the girl needs to be in pre-kindergarten. That's the law, and noncompliance will force me to report you for child neglect and have the children removed from your custody and placed in foster care. You being a big shot commissioner and about the richest guy in the county will not give you the right to do as you like.

"Dave, you try anything like that, and you will have to contend with my attorney. As I understand it, pre-kindergarten is voluntary. And if the district has a teacher who is fluent in Russian, I will consider sending my son to school. In the meantime, he will be home schooled. Now, get the hell out of my home."

"You will hear from us again and here is your citation You have been served..." With that they slammed the front door behind them.

They had not even left the ranch yet, when Cliff was on the line to Oscar Niewalder, his attorney, and told him what had happened. "Do something to make this go away" were his last words, before he hung up the phone.

The end result of that visit was, however, that Sasha had to start school. He was by then fairly comfortable with English. He was excited to go. Now, he was a big boy. He no longer had to take a nap. He was almost a grown up now.

It was Rina, who had the most trouble with Sasha going to school. She had always been with him, wherever they had been. Now, for the first time, she was on her own. She had no playmate anymore. The Garza grandchildren were too old to play with her. Besides, they too, went to school. Katja had a very hard time keeping her daughter entertained and busy.

She too had things on her mind. She must learn to drive that big vehicle, so she could take Sasha to school and pick him up again. Right now, he was taking the school bus with the Garza grandchildren, but Cliff had to pick him up, for he went to school only half a day. Besides that, he did not like for the little guy to walk down to the county road in the dark and wait there for the school bus to arrive in the cold.

Toward the end of February, a long letter arrived from Russia. Tatiana had gotten everyone together, and all had contributed to that epistle. Everyone was happy for her, and they missed her. They also forwarded what mail she had received. Everyone found what she had told them in her letters unbelievable. Tatiana told her, she was seriously thinking of taking her own chance and advertising once again. She had no responses the last time, but perhaps, she would be lucky this time. They all thanked her for the clothing she had sent, and the small gifts she had sent them for Christmas. Tatiana could not believe that those stunning earrings should not have cost a fortune. She had several offers to purchase them from some of the more prosperous ladies in town. No, she was not parting with her gift.

Among her mail were the last paychecks still outstanding from the railway. Another letter contained the determination from the courts about her widow benefits and those for the children. She would receive two checks in the future for each of them, one each from the railroad and another from the Chernobyl Nuclear Commission. There were also checks for the amount of back pay owed her and the children. Katja immediately wrote to Olga to ask her to forward future letters to her and another to all the agencies involved with a change of address. She was just not sure if they would forward in the future the checks to America. On her next visit to town, she tried to open an account at the local bank to deposit all the funds she had received but was informed that it would be better if she deposited the funds at a big city bank. So, on the monthly visit to Amarillo, she visited the First National Bank and made arrangements for her own account.

She was advised she would not be able to access the funds for some time in the future, until they had cleared the banking system. The savings counselor promised to mail a notice when that happened. Three months later, the payments started to arrive at fairly regular intervals. One evening Katja confided to Cliff that she was glad it had taken the authorities such a long time to make their decision, for if the money had arrived while she still was in Russia, she would never have come. That would have been awful, for she would never have known the kind of happiness she had now.

As a result of the letters from her friends in Russia, Katja thought she would go through the children's clothing again and ship what was too small back to her friend, Tatiana. Maybe she would be able to sell them and so make a few extra *Kopeks*. She might be able to add an item or two for her friend's use.

When spring break came in March, the family went to Oklahoma City for the entire week. Cliff had safety meetings with the County Commissioners Association, but the women had activities also. There was the visit to the Zoo, and the Cowboy Hall of Fame and Museum. There was the Kirkpatrick Planetarium for a day's entertainment and, of course, Frontier City amusement park. In the evenings, they had dinner in Bricktown, and they rode the boats along the canal.

All the ladies in the organization took Katja and her children under their wings, trying to show them a great time, and included them in all the activities. Katja was totally astonished by all the new friends she was making. She knew that back in Russia, she would have never been included in the affairs of what she thought of as leaders. On their way back home, Cliff stopped at the biggest gun store in town and purchased two huge gun safes. Katja could not imagine what they might be for.

Once home, Cliff installed the gun safes in the tornado shelter. He had solved at least part of the problem of what to do with the Russian antiques. Katja could not comprehend his concern. He was afraid an intruder might steal them, or a tornado might damage or destroy them. In the cellar in a locked safe, they would be secure, at least until he heard from Sotheby's on how to care for them. He was still convinced they should be in a museum. He did, however, allow Katja to display the paintings and the icons, and he had her put the eggs into a display case in the dining room, under lock and key.

Easter was just around the corner and the children had picked up on the Easter Bunny. That was another holiday with which Katja was not familiar. She tried to make the holiday a Russian Easter, like her parents had told her about. But during her lifetime, the day had not been celebrated under the Communist regime, and afterward, the people had forgotten about the day, like so many other religious celebrations.

The colored eggs and soft fluffy bunnies were a great hit with the children. Even Sasha was glad for the little long eared bunny he received and slept with it at night. Rina's bed was full of stuffed critters that all slept with her. There were so many, she hardly had space on that big bed to stretch out completely. She was happy, nestled among all her furry friends
.

Sasha's sixth birthday was the week after Easter. Cliff told Katja to make it a very special celebration for Sasha. She tried to tell him that the child does not need another celebration, there had been too many already.

"No, Katja, in America the children invite all their friends to help them open their presents and to have cake and ice cream. There have to be six candles on the cake. We will order a big sheet cake for the occasion from the bakery in town. Afterwards, the children will play and have lots of fun for about two hours, and then their parents come and pick them up again. Usually, there is also a little celebration in school. So be prepared for that."

"I guess, he can invite one or two little boys that he likes a lot from school. That would be all right, don't you think?"

"No, Katja, invite his whole class There are only about twelve children in that class. Everyone should come. We'll pick up invitation cards at the Walmart and write into them all the particulars about the party, and he can hand them out in school to all the children."

"You want him to invite twelve children to this house?" Katja was incredulous. "They will wreck your beautiful house. So many children are uncontrollable."

"We will manage. I'll be here to help you, and so will Inez and Donna and maybe Don can come too, if he gets the chance. He will impress the children, and they will be on their best behavior. Just wait and see." Cliff was chuckling. Katja was appalled. Donna explained that they should obtain small party favors for all the kids. Katja did not know what that was. She was even more surprised, when it was explained to her, that one gives little gifts to all the attending children.

"You have to give the invited children presents for coming to a party. Don't they give presents to the birthday child? Not that Sasha needs any more presents; his room is about full, and not another thing will fit. And such an expense!" Katja was absolutely incredulous.

"Don't worry so. It will not be that expensive. You just give a small something. You spend very little money, maybe a dollar or two on the gift for each child. Maybe a few Crayolas, or a little bauble, just something, a pretty pencil. That sort of thing." Donna tried to explain. Katja looked helplessly at Cliff for a better understanding. She was sure that she had not understood what everyone was telling her.

"Sweetie, you better think about the present we will surprise the boy with. Something he has his heart set on, but does not think he will ever get. By the way, he needs a summer straw hat among other things. Can the children swim?"

"No, I don't think so. The river at home was too cold to bathe in. Maybe they can splash in that river down there or in one of the ponds on the ranch.

That might be fun for all of us," she conceded.

"No, dear. That will never do. I don't know what kind of snakes are in the ponds, but a few cottonmouths for sure. No they have to have a pool, out there in the back yard."

"You are kidding me, a pool? I have never even heard of such a thing. Maybe in the gym in Yekaterinburg there is a pool, but not in our small village. Nobody had a pool there. I am sure of that. No, such a thing does not exist. Not a pool for just a couple of kids. Maybe in the bigger towns, there are pools for the children of the town to enjoy, but never ever a pool for just one family. I cannot imagine such a thing."

"Well, we don't have to have it right away, and it does not have to be an Olympic sized pool, but a little one for swimming laps. That would be so much fun. Skinny dipping on a hot summer night is not so bad, and the kids sure would like it on a hot summer afternoon. We don't have to have an inground pool but an above ground version would surely be nice. I've been thinking about one ever since I moved into this place. Let's think about it."

Katja was speechless. "What is this skinny dipping?" When that was explained to her, she blushed. Donna confided, she just might come and join the children in the pool on a hot summer afternoon. Don, too, was not averse to a plunge into cool water.

Only nine of the twelve children in Aleksandr's class came to the party, and they behaved so well, Katja was astounded. Even little Irina was included in all their games, and there were several girls amongst the guests, who loved playing with her dolls and doll house. Everyone had brought a small gift for Sasha, coloring books, and activity books, a huge box of Crayolas, a book for reading.

Several of the mothers volunteered to help clean up after the party, but surprisingly, everything was under control. Katja had never experienced paper plates, napkins and tablecloths. Cliff brought a trash can in, and the children all discarded their paper and plastic ware, once they were finished with cake and ice cream. Once the children were playing outside, he scooped up the discarded wrapping, and the house was back to order. Afterward Katja confessed to him,

"I thought this party would be so much trouble. But all the children were so nice, and nobody got into a fight or made a mess. What well behaved children American children are. This party was so much fun; we must do the same when Rina has her birthday. Is that acceptable?"

"Most certainly. She will have so much fun. I just wish we knew more people with children her age. She needs playmates. She is so lonesome."

"Yes, I agree. But we live so far from neighbors, so she cannot have friends. Is okay, she is with me." Katja tried to prevent him from being concerned.

"Let me think about that for a while. I think we will be able to figure something out."

Chapter Sixteen

After Katja finally had her driver's license, it was decided that three days a week, Irina would be enrolled in a day care center for half a day, while Sasha was in school. Katja would drop the children off in the morning and pick them up at noon. She would have a few hours to herself, where she might go to the beauty salon, or do some shopping in town, or just visit with friends. She would be able to meet other women, when she dropped off and picked up the children. Perhaps, she could make a friend, like she had in Russia.

Slowly, Katja and the children became

302

acclimated to America. The weather was now warmer than what they had ever experienced. She could finally see the need for summer clothing and perhaps also for the swimming pool. She still could not understand the need for insurance for her family's heirlooms, and the tornado threat was totally incomprehensible to her. Cliff watched the late news every night and the weather channel. He tried to show her pictures of tornado damage. Katja just could not fathom that a little bit of wind could do such damage. *No,* she thought, *the government must have exploded a new weapon and failed to inform the people. It happened all the time in Russia.*

Sasha had come home from school one day and had told everyone over lunch that they had a fire drill at school that day, and they had also practiced what to do in case of a tornado. He explained to his mother that they might also want to practice that here at home, for he did not wish for his little sister to be caught unaware of what to do. Cliff thought it a splendid idea, and so after lunch they practiced getting into the tornado shelter the quickest way possible. They even focused on what to bring with them. Katja was ambivalent about the exercise, and so participated only halfheartedly.

The days were beautiful and balmy toward the first part of May. School would be out in a couple of more weeks, and Sasha was all excited about summer vacation and what adventures he would have. Cliff was busy in the pastures and barns with new calves and colts. Katja was getting ready for her first solo trip to Amarillo the following Monday. Inez would take care of the children. She was sitting at the table in the breakfast area, making lists of what was needed from what store. The children needed sandals, and so did she. They all needed several shorts and light tops. Even Cliff had asked her to buy him some at the Big and Tall store in Amarillo.

Then there was the endless list of groceries she once again needed. She was trying to figure out how much money she might need to take along. The sum seemed enormous to her, especially since she was still converting everything into Rubles. She tried to slash extraneous items, but there was not much she could delete. She was almost despondent by the amount of money she would have to spend. Cliff did not seem to be concerned. He had told her to take along several ice chests to stow the perishables on the way home.

She was getting up to get herself another glass of tea and to check the reserves in the pantry, when she noticed a huge, roiling, ominous, black cloud, coming in from the northwest. It had obscured the sun completely. She checked on the children. Sasha was upstairs, playing computer games, and Rina should be taking a nap, but lately, more often than not, she was playing quietly in her room with her cat.

Outside, there was, for once, no wind, only the threatening clouds, only those menacing clouds racing towards her. It would be raining any minute now. This morning, when she had tried to hang up clothes to dry, they just hung there, limp and wet. She had been bathed in perspiration and had taken another cool shower, just to cool off again, when she came in from hanging up the wash. She should have put all of it in the dryer, but she liked the smell of clothes that had been dried in the sunshine. And such sunshine as here in America had never been experienced by her in the Ural Mountains of Siberian Russia.

Suddenly, it started raining as if the sluice gates of heaven had been opened, the sky and earth merged as if one. Cliff burst into the house, the dog at his heels.

"Katja, into the cellar now! Where are the kids?"

She told him. He hollered for the boy while he scooped up Rina and the cat. Katja was already out of the door, her purse slung over her shoulder. She had suddenly realized, that this was indeed, very dangerous. Cliff handed her Rina and the cat and then ran back for the boy. By that time, Sasha was most of the way down the stairs. Cliff snatched up the child and was at the cellar an instant later.

By this time the noise from the storm was deafening. Hail splattered on the roof; a window broke somewhere in the house. Sasha was scooting down the stairs. Cliff shoved the dog after him. Then he, too, was on his way down, trying at the same time to close the heavy hatch door behind him. He had a hard time. The wind was trying to slam it back open. With Katja clinging to his legs, he was finally able to secure it.

They were all glad for the few things he had placed down there for creature comfort; A few lawn chairs, so everyone could sit, and a blanket for each of them was there as well as a several of bottles of water, a few flashlights and a battery-operated radio. He was most happy that all of the irreplaceable Russian heirlooms were securely residing in his gun safes in the cellar.

His cell phone was riding in his belt. Cliff knew that they had been hit. He tried to prepare his family for that. They could not comprehend that. When it finally seemed quiet above, Cliff attempted to open the hatch. It would not budge. The cell phone did not work. They were below ground after all, and the nearest tower was quite a ways away. The radio reported widespread and severe damage to Boise City and the surrounding county.

Finally, Cliff was able to make a call, while perching on the ladder as close to the hatch as he could get. He was able to contact his friend, the Sheriff, and tell him of their predicament.

After a long time, they finally heard noises, and the hatch was opened. Outside, the sun was shining. the storm had passed and taken their wonderful house with it. Only rubble existed where once it had stood.

They were all stunned. Katja and the children were hysterical. He could not let them grieve like that. Right now, they had to find what was salvageable and make arrangements for the night. Surprisingly, the few Russian antiques still in the house were safe. Things that had been inside of cupboards and drawers had remained intact. The second story, however was totally gone. The ceilings were missing, and the furniture in the larger rooms were gone. What furniture did remain was soggy and wet, the same for the carpets. The vehicles were damaged severely under a cover of the collapsed roof and ceiling.

To rescue the family, a forklift had to be brought in. Even before Cliff had been able to contact the Sheriff, Jorge had been able to call for help. He had been trying to get to them out alone, but had been unable to lift the heavy timbers off the hatch by himself.

The house was a total loss; they could not even remain in it for the night. Surprisingly, the outbuildings, barn, and the old house had damage but were useable.

Inez and Jorge as well as their children were there helping to collect Cliff and Katja's belongings.

Don could not help. He had other worries, and Donna was trying to patch up their own house. Cliff tried to make arrangements to spend the next few nights at the motel in town. The motel was booked to capacity by the time he was able to call. They would have to go to Texas or to Guymon. Inez came to the rescue. They would stay with them in the old house, until other arrangements could be made.

They all worked hard for the remaining hours of daylight. Any salvaged useable belongings were being stored in the barn and tack room. It was surprising how many of their belongings were found, much of it scattered over a wide area of the ranch, all of it soaking wet. But clothes could be washed again, and papers would be spread out and dried again, even photographs were being collected and laid flat to dry in the barn. Jorge was checking on the livestock and came back reporting good news. They had lost none of their animals. Most of the furniture, however, was damaged beyond redemption.

From the first moment Sasha had crawled out of the shelter, and he had realized how ruined everything was, he was afraid for Billie, his pony. The child was glad that Snowball had been with them in the shelter and was safe, but Billie had been out in the pasture, and the child was sure the pony was hurt or missing. So once released from the shelter, he attempted to race and check on his pony. Jorge caught him, just before the boy tripped over a piece of roofing. The older man was trying to reassure the child that the little horse was fine and grazing. No, Sasha had to see for himself. Katja was too distraught to even see what the boy was up to, but Cliff had noticed, and he was happy to see that the child cared so much for his animal.

Next, he needed to reassure Katja, telling her they would rebuild the house. That is why they had insurance, but Katja could not comprehend that. She was sure her dream home was gone forever, and she would once again have to live in cramped quarters, just like in Russia. It was incomprehensible for her that everything could and would be replaced. She walked around, deeply shocked finding the most insignificant possessions, while totally ignoring what was important.

Theirs, of course, was not the only building damaged in town or in the county. The school was heavily damaged, and school was declared out for the summer. By fall, the authorities hoped to have everything repaired, the teacher told Katja when she inquired a couple of days later. There were many residences, businesses, and public buildings damaged in town.

The insurance company provided the Collins family a trailer house as temporary housing, since no apartments or houses were available in town for sale or rent, until such a time as their home could be rebuilt. Katja had a hard time understanding that they would rebuild, bigger and better even, to her liking and to her wishes. That was unfathomable to her, a house built to her specifications! Cliff had a hard time convincing her of that. It was hard for her to understand that they were not living in the tuna can forever. Eventually, she did start drawing floorplans of how she thought the new home might be laid out.

They had been so lucky. No one was hurt, and none of the livestock had been lost, but the fences were down in many places, and Jorge and Cliff spent many a day out on the range mending fences.

They had just moved into the trailer when Sasha became seriously ill. Katja was afraid his father's compromised genes were putting the boy's life in danger. That was not the case. Sasha had a severe respiratory infection, picked up at school from another child, but he had an extremely high fever, and he had to spend most of a week in hospital in Amarillo.

The boy was still recuperating at home, when Katja found out she was pregnant. She had not wanted to tell Cliff until she was sure, but he figured it out, when she was sick, morning after morning. He was delighted. He took her to the doctor right away, and both were surprised when they were told she was carrying twins. When asked if there had ever been twins in her family by the doctor, she had to admit that her grandfather had been a twin.

Chapter Seventeen

N̲ow, the planning for the new house started in earnest. It would have to be larger than the old house. They needed a large nursery with a bath, and a room that could be converted to a bedroom, once the babies had grown enough. Cliff also wanted his office again on the ground floor, and the tornado shelter should be larger to accommodate the entire family.

While in Amarillo, they drove around the newer neighborhoods, to give Katja an idea of building styles and exterior looks, stucco, brick, rock, Texas sandstone, clapboard, etc. She found that she liked a combination of stucco and Texas sandstone. Cliff too, liked the look. Donnie, Don, and Donna's son, was called in to design the new McMansion. This time, he had no trouble convincing Cliff of some of the newer features.

Hollis Webber, the builder from Guymon, came over as soon as he was requested. While Donnie was still in Boise City, the plans for the new home was being finalized. So, a little more than a month after the disaster, the new building plans had been completed.

Katja was in awe of the speed with which all of this had taken place. She hoped that by the time the babies were a year old, they would be in their new home. That was not Cliff's plan. He knew he would not live that long in a sardine can, no matter that it was a nice double wide with three bedrooms and a large living area. It was still a tin can. He hated it. Katja thought she would have been delighted to have such a fine home in Russia. It was hard for her to imagine, that it had not been built on site, but that it was trucked in and had wheels. Such a thing was really not fathomable.

Such homes did not exist in Russia, but here the home was, and she was living in it. In her letter to Tatiana, she tried to describe her new abode and even included some pictures, one of which showed the wheels. The answer that came back, had her laughing too, for her friend was convinced, Cliff had placed the wheels strategically against the building to fool Katja's friend. Tatiana wistfully thought that both she and Olga would be delighted to live in such a fine home and not in one dark room, as they both were.

Life was hectic that summer, for not only did

she have to go to Amarillo monthly for supplies, she also went several times to have a look into the furniture stores. She found some things she liked but remembered that she had seen in the stores in Santa Fe the very distinctive furniture in the Santa Fe, New Mexico, style. So, the week before school started the whole family went for a few days to New Mexico, to see what was available there. Katja loved what she found. They made arrangements for the store decorator to work with her, to come to the ranch, and have a look at the building, once the place was mostly completed.

Two days after their return, Sasha started first grade, a momentous occasion in his young life. Soon, he would be able to write to his friend Sergey himself and not have to ask his mother to write for him. He was looking forward to that. He had this huge goal, and so he worked particularly diligently to learn to read and write. It was soon apparent that he had mastered far more than his classmates, and during a teacher parent conference, the possibility of his being advanced to second grade ahead of schedule was being discussed. The decision was that he remain with his class, for it was only in this one area of the curriculum that he was ahead. He needed to be more comfortable with his other class work. Sasha's friend Sergey too, had entered the first grade a couple of months earlier.

Little Irina was once again enrolled in day care. She too had made friends, and was looking forward to playing with them again. The time at daycare taught her many things, and she improved her English tremendously. Katja too had made some friends with the mothers of some of the children in Irina's playgroup. Several of Irina's playmates had lost also their homes to the tornado, or the homes had been damaged enough to not be habitable until repairs could be made.

Katja had learned that some of her acquaintances had had to move in with relatives or in-laws. She felt for these women and counted her blessings, knowing how much worse the disaster was affecting these people. She commiserated with them, and she took one of the ladies along on her next shopping trip to Amarillo, for that young woman did not have a vehicle of her own but needed to shop for summer clothing for her family and also stop by and purchase linen and such, for she had lost literally everything she had owned in the tornado.

For Katja, the time alone was needed not only to rest, but to get ready for the new babies. Besides planning the new house, she also had a nursery to get ready for the new arrivals. Rina was looking forward to the babies; they would be playmates for her. She was sure, she was going to have at least one little sister. Sasha was hoping for boys, but Rina had always been correct when predicting future events, so he did not fasten all his hopes on a little brother.

The family was happy and watching with

wonder the progress of the building of their new home. During all that time, items they had lost in the tornado showed up in unexpected places. Almost daily a friend, acquaintance, or neighbor came by or called to report they had found one or more lost possessions. One day, towards the middle of September, a rancher called to say he had found a box, which he thought might contain computer disks, he thought might belong to Cliff. The box was locked and dented, still tight and not open. He had stumbled across the metal container in a far pasture he seldom used, while making hay. Would Cliff please come over and have a look at it?

When Cliff came back from the run to that rancher a good twenty-five miles away, he was smiling and carrying the little gray metal box under his arm.

"This is great, Katja. I got all my records back, All the tax records for the last few years, the records of what each well is producing, and the proceeds and all the breeding records for the livestock. I invited the rancher and his wife for an evening at the club on Friday. You will like the couple, I am sure. They are young and are having a tough time. A night out will be a treat for them, and they saved us so much time and money, I cannot even explain it all to you. From now on, I will leave a copy of all my files in the tornado shelter. They really are almost impossible to replace."

For once, Katja had no trouble agreeing with

him. The experience of the last months had given her a healthy respect for a tornado. She would never again call a tornado just a little wind.

Katja did like the young couple. She had a wonderful time with the young wife, and she invited her along on her next shopping trip to Amarillo. Here was a young woman only a little younger than herself, with similar interests and challenges as Katja's.

They became fast friends. Even their children became playmates for Rina and Sasha. Sasha already knew the boy from school, and he developed into a real pal for him. Here was a boy, he could tell all about his life in Russia and of his friends over there, that he missed so much. Rina and Kylie became fast friends too, and many an afternoon, the two little girls could be found playing together in her room with her dolls, while their mothers were working together on special projects.

Cliff told Katja that she might write her friends, if it might be possible for them that they should ship some of her furniture over and for that to be used in the new house. He had seen some of the items in her pictures, and they seemed to be wonderful. Katja tried to demure. The upholstery was so bad, that she thought they should be discarded.

"No, Sweets, I'd like for you to have some of what you treasure here. Besides, upholstery can be replaced. Dick and Frances Walker have a wonderful upholstery shop in town. You can pick the fabrics you like. I am sure the decorator will help you too, in deciding what you should choose." They sent that letter and promised to send the money needed. Cliff was going to ask the Mayflower Moving company in Amarillo the next time he was in town, how to best accomplish that job.

The next morning, even before five o'clock, Katja woke with labor pains. She could at first not believe it, thinking she had just eaten something that did not agree with her, but when she started spotting, Cliff called the doctor instantly. The old doc had passed a few years ago, the one who had taken care of Mary, but his son Johnny had taken over the practice. He was a good kid and a competent doctor. He had called the helicopter on his way out to the ranch. This time, Cliff was able to ride along in the chopper. Inez had taken over with the children, and Jorge had promised to pick them up in the SUV as soon as Katja was ready to come home.

This time, the doctors were able to stop the labor, but Katja was going to have to stay in the hospital for the duration of her pregnancy. Cliff spend several days with her, until the greatest danger was over. Donna came and got him, when it was time for him to go back home. While in Amarillo, he had rented a vehicle and had visited the movers and made arrangements to have the furniture shipped from Russia, without telling Katja about it. He had called Russia and been able to talk to both Olga and Tatiana one night and had asked them to please ship all the furniture that had once belonged to the dacha. Tatiana had explained that there were several very nice pieces, she knew of, in the homes of some of the villagers. Should they try to buy them also?

"You know that will be expensive, but I think Katja would be so pleased. She was always upset, when she found out about another piece, that had once belonged to her family and had been taken away, while her father was in the Gulag."

Cliff was surprised to hear that. "I did not know her dad had been in the Gulag. She never said anything about that."

"Oh, he was not so much detained. He just had to sleep there for many years, he was even allowed to take his dog and cat along. When Stalin rounded up everyone he thought might be from the old regime, Nicolay Petrovitch had to go too.

But he had made friends with the commander long ago, providing him fresh vegetables and dairy products that he was raising alone on the old estate. Yosip Leonidov did not want to lose his source of good produce, so he allowed Katja's father to continue with his farm while in the Gulag.

He also befriended Marina Standinova, who eventually become his wife and was the mother of Katja. When under Khrushchev, the reins were loosened, he once again returned to the dacha. Only by this time, the best rooms had been occupied by others, so he took up the old servant quarters and furnished them with some of the furniture he had hidden away. No one knows where that is, except perhaps Katja. She and her father were uncommonly close, and old Nicolay instilled in her, her love for her family."

"I did not know any of this, but then we have had so much to learn of each other, that there really has not been any time to discuss all of the family. I did know she was extremely close to her father and misses him still.

"So, those family furniture pieces might be bought, did you not say that?"

"Da, Miester Collins. Will cost many Rubbles, can you send?"

"Of course, would Dollars be better? Would they make it easier for you to convince the people to part with those things?"

"Is possible, da, I think so. Is good idea."

"How much money would you need, Tatiana? Do you have an idea? I want those things here when Katja comes home from the hospital with the babies. I also want the house to be finished by then. I have already told the builder the house will have to be finished in three month. I can wire you the funds."

"No, not telegram, then we get money in Rubbles. You have to send money in letter, and small bills. I cannot change Dollars in Novorotskoye. This way, I can say I have only so few Dollars and no more. People will sell, and not charge too much, is old stuff, after all." Tatiana thought maybe five hundred Dollars would buy all there was.

The next morning Cliff went to the bank and withdrew two thousand dollars in small bills, nothing bigger than a ten Dollar bill. The bank had to scramble. In the meantime, he found a nice *Air Bourne* small box and wrote a long letter to Katja's friends.

That same day, he made the arrangements to have the Katja's furniture and other belongings picked up by the movers in Russia, no later than six weeks from that day. He mailed the money and letter package that some evening, via Air Borne the quickest delivery possible. He had asked Tatiana to please call him once the package arrived to confirm delivery. Three days later, she called to say the money had safely arrived, and the movers had already contacted Olga to inquire how much furniture was going out. Tatiana also thanked him for the huge amount of money. She was sure she would not need all of it: she was going to return the remainder.

Three weeks later, she called to say she had

purchased every last item they had found in the village. Not only had she found furniture, but some china, linen, paintings, and other art objects, all items had the emblem of the Novorotsky family someplace affixed or incorporated into the design. They would also send all the books Katja had inherited from her father. She still had just under one thousand Dollars left. Everything was being crated that day and would be shipped by tomorrow evening. She was including the money in the shipment in a small container inside the desk from Katja's rooms.

"No, Tatiana, keep the money and give some to Olga and Oleg, who have helped you so much with this project. Please do not mention any of this to Katja in your letters. It is a surprise for her for when she comes home from the hospital. Our new home will be ready by then."

"No *Miester* Collins, I cannot take so much money for so little I do for my friend."

"Yes, you can. Have a little fun, buy you what you need. Katja would love for you to have it."

"Miester Collins, have big favor to ask. Can you please send for Olga; she is so lonesome for her little bird and Sasha and Katja? I think she is getting sick. Maybe Katja need help with two babies, Olga would be good. I will give her all the money, for her fare, is ok?"

"That is a great idea, and yes, Katja will need

help. But don't spend your money. I will make the arrangements. There are some problems with immigration, I have to clear up first. I will call Olga, when all is ready. But tell her please, to prepare to come over here in the next few months. If she needs money to clear up her affairs, have her let me know how much she needs and also, if she is willing to come."

"She is right here. She wants to tell you. Is okay?"

"She is there? I would love to talk to her, can you translate?"

"Da."

In very broken English, an older voice said to Cliff. "Da, I come, soon. Is good, da, Miesta Cliff."

"Great! Katja will be so happy." Then he told Tatiana to have Olga include any of her belongings that she wanted to retain, to ship them with their things. He would try to have her over long before Katja was out of the hospital.

And so, it was all arraigned. Cliff called the builder and asked him to add servant's quarters to the side of the house, two rooms and a bath and a large closet, and to have all of that ready at the same time as the house.

"Where do you want those rooms? In the attic?"

"No, I guess the best place would be on the other side of the garages, with a separate entrance from the outside and maybe a little terrace of its own too. Yeah, I think that would work. I want her to have some privacy."

Katja spent the remainder of her pregnancy in the hospital. She was able to get up and sit in a comfortable recliner, some of the time. She was allowed to use the bathroom, and even take a shower, but only with a nurse in attendance.

She was able to work with the decorator from her hospital room, and was able to make the decision concerning what furniture to purchase and what hardware to use throughout the house. She was involved with selecting the color scheme for the house and the rooms, but she had no knowledge of the furniture, that would be arriving from Russia or of her friend coming.

Donna helped her with outfitting the nursery. She came twice a month, and with the list Katja had compiled and what she thought the young mother would need and want, the nursery was taking shape. During the last two weeks, she was not even allowed out of the bed anymore. A bedpan and sponge baths had to suffice.

The babies were born on the second of December, about two weeks earlier than expected. The doctors decided it would be best if the babies would be born by Caesarian section. That way, they did not have to undergo so much trauma, and it would be easier on Katja, also. The babies were two tiny little girls, Nadja Marie and Helena Marishka.

Helena was extremely small and underdeveloped and died within a couple of days of birth. The loss of the little girl devastated both Cliff and Katja. They buried her in the cemetery out on highway 287 at the edge of town. Having little Nadja was not so much a consolation, but a reminder of what they had lost. Still, they doted on her for all her life, afraid, every little cold might kill her, and she was frail for many years, but later, in her teen years, she became a robust young girl and beautiful, just like her older sister. Rina adored her little sister. They were inseparable for most of their lives.

Three days later, Katja could have gone home, but the house was not quite finished. Everyone was working feverishly, even Olga, who had arrived by plane in Amarillo the previous week and had been installed in the room with little Irina. Cliff conspired with Doctor Johnnie to have Katja stay in the hospital for another week to recover her strength, and get the use of her legs back. So Katja stayed in the hospital until her little daughter was ready to go home, too.

The Russian furniture had arrived just a week

previously, and Olga immediately started to polish and clean all of it. The decorator had found fabric that would enhance all the upholstered pieces, and had instructed the couple who was doing the work to have it finished in record time. When the decorator saw all the Russian heirloom pieces she congratulated Cliff on being able to have brought over all this museum quality furniture. She told him every last piece was priceless. She even helped Olga when she was polishing all that wonderful wood.

For Katja's arrival home, the house looked fabulous. Olga was happy as a clam and could hardly wait to greet and welcome her friend home. When Rina and Sasha saw all their old belongings being unpacked, they started dancing around the house. Now this was really home. Sasha only hoped that soon he would be able to greet his friend Sergey here in America too. Rina was a happy little bird in the company of her old friend. She knew her Mama would be so happy to have all of them together again.

When Katja finally arrived home, Cliff took her first into the nursery. The second crib had been removed, and only the old cradle that had held all the Novorotsky children was there. Katja was dumbfounded and could not express her gratefulness fully for finding the family cradle ready for her little daughter. She had been surprised to see the house complete When they arrived at the ranch, the trailer was gone already. It was as if the tornado had never happened, only the new house was so much bigger and nicer. She had not noticed the addition to the side of the house that held the little apartment for Olga.

Baby Nadja was tired, and Cliff urged his wife to put her down. He was bursting at the seams to show her all the other surprises.

"Come, Sweetheart, let me show you the rest of the house. The baby will be fine. I know the others missed you so much and are waiting to hug you."

"Yes, I've missed them too, but are they not in school today?"

"Not most of the day. Donna went and got them a little while ago. They should be home by now. Come." He guided her into the living room. And there they all were, Don and Donna and Jorge and Inez and their children and Sasha and Irina on either side of Olga, who was grinning. Katja was speechless, at first.

"Olga, you came, when? Why you not come to hospital? How long can you stay?"

"Mr. Cliff want to surprise you. There was so much to do here, to have house ready for you and baby. Where is baby?"

"She is sleeping. Come, I want to show you my little girl."

"Let her sleep a little while, till you have seen all, Katja. Mr. Cliff said I can stay here. He even built me my own apartment. No longer must I live in just one room and share kitchen and bath. I have my own." Olga told her friend very proudly.

"Welcome home!" everyone was yelling and clamoring for Katja's attention. But seeing her friend, and some of her old furniture had Katja's attention first. Katja laughed and cried and hugged and kissed them all. But for Cliff, there was a special thank you. She did not know how to do it, if she was able to make him understand how happy she was, but he knew. He saw it in her smile, in her eyes, in her happiness.

"I hope you don't mind, Sweetheart, but I asked Olga to come and live with us, to help you with the house and the children, to be a substitute grandmother for them. Is that all right with you?" She did not even have time to respond, for then, they all mobbed her and hugged her and kissed her, and she walked through her new home as if in a dream.

She finally was able to see all the Russian belongings, even some of which she had not been aware. Olga was telling her how Tatiana and Oleg and she had convinced the folks. who had absconded with her families' heirlooms, to return them and how Cliff had made all of it possible.

The children did not want to let go of her. Finally, everyone settled down, and Olga was making a late lunch for all of them. Once little Nadja woke from her nap, everyone cooed over the new baby, and then the friends all left for their own homes. Olga would not let Katja do anything for the remainder of the day.

Once Cliff left to check on the livestock, Katja and Olga settled down for a long talk and all the news from her hometown.

"Tatiana too is hoping to visit for a little while in the coming months." Olga confided. "Even Oleg was thinking about it. Life for him in Russia was no fun anymore without his friend Olga. My rooms are big enough for both of us, if Mr. Cliff will allow it. He too can help with the ranch, if Mr. Cliff needs more help. He works so very hard.

"Last winter was so cold at home, Oleg lost one of his horses. Now he has just the one, and that is not enough to support him. He can sell that horse, and come here too. He would like that. It is not so cold there. I have not seen snow since I am here, and it is January. We need so little, and with the pension, we can have sent here, we could make it together. That would be so good.

"Oh, Madame Bulin, has been beaten by her man friend very badly, and he is now in prison in Yekaterinburg. Sergey and Elena have been taken away by the government and placed in an orphanage. I hope that he is able to write to Sasha."

And so, they talked, until it was time for supper. This time, Katja insisted on making it. She wanted a meal that she knew Cliff would like especially. She wanted to prepare his favorite. Later, Olga proudly showed Katja her little apartment. It was at least twice the size of what she had lived in at the dacha. Even here were a few of the old pieces from the dacha. When packing up all the books still in the old library, they had found the escape route, that her father had kept secret, and so they found all the furniture still stored away. All of that had been shipped to America. Olga told Katja that nothing of the Novorotsky belongings remained at the dacha. It had all been shipped to America.

Later that evening, when she and Cliff were alone in their bedroom, he told her how he had managed to get it all. Now, every room in the house held at least one piece of her furniture. They walked hand in hand all through the house, and Katja finally was able to absorb what all was there, and how clever the decorator had been to incorporate all of it into an American home. Some pieces had been slightly altered to give them a different purpose, but none of the beauty had been affected. Katja almost did not recognize the upholstered pieces, even though she had been sitting in one of the chairs all afternoon.

When she finally went to bed, she told Cliff, that she could not remember ever being this happy. She never had expected to be this loved, and she would never, ever want to be without him again. She fell asleep nestled in his arms. That is how she wanted to always go to sleep for the rest of her days. This was total happiness, something Katja had never expected to experience, something she had not known existed. This was a happiness she would never have known, had she remained in Russia.

Cliff too was happy. He, too, had never expected to be this happy. He had hoped for another mate but could not imagine that person would be making him as happy as what Mary had. Katja did that and more. He loved her more than what he was able to express. He, too, wanted to go to sleep every night, for the rest of his life, with Katja nestled in his arms. He, too, realized how lucky he was to have found her.

The End

ABOUT THE AUTHOR

Rosemarie Sabel Durgin is German by birth and come to this country as a young mother. She has been a Naturalized Citizen since 1966. She is the mother of four and grandmother of ten.

She and her husband live in Bethany, Oklahoma with a menagerie of dogs and cats.

Rosemarie enjoys reading and writing, now that she is retired. She also likes to do needlework of any kind and photography of wildlife. She loves traveling in the American West.

Her next novel will be about two young German women who came to America in the mid 1800's and became pioneers. They were 'Women, Immigrants and Pioneers'. Look for the book at your favorite bookstore or on Amazon.com.